Life's Lessons

(Living and Loving Leaving No Stone Unturned)

Kimberly Perry Allen

Jacqueline Goodwin

Teena Saunders

BK

ROYSTON
Publishing

BK Royston Publishing
P. O. Box 4321
Jeffersonville, IN 47131
502-802-5385
http://www.bkroystonpublishing.com
bkroystonpublishing@gmail.com

Cover Design: Elite Cover Designs
Back Cover Photo: Alice Beck

ISBN-13: 978-1-959543-93-0

King James Version Scriptural Text – Public Domain

New International Version - NIV - Holy Bible, New
International Version®, NIV® Copyright ©1973, 1978, 1984,
2011 by Biblica, Inc.® Used by permission. All rights reserved
worldwide.

Printed in the United States of America

DEDICATION

To all survivors: We are hard pressed on every side, but not crushed; perplexed, but not in despair; persecuted, but not abandoned; struck down, but not destroyed.

2 Corinthians 4:8-9 (NIV)

Thanks to my family and friends for their love and patience in this endeavor. **Jacque**

A special thanks to my parents, children, and grandchildren. Thank you to my sister circle for your love and encouragement. **Kim**

Dedicated to my mother Brenda Martin. **Teena**

Special Thanks

Thank you Pastor Jamaal Williams for your guidance, support, and prayer covering.

Table of Contents

Introduction

Life's Lessons (Living and Loving Leaving No Stone Unturned) is a debut novel and collaborative writing piece that was roused by the tone of recent reconciliation and healing in light of the racial tension that presented itself across the country several years ago.

This story was inspired by true events that take place in a small town in Kentucky.

Hushed and kept silent no more, four older African American women befriend a much younger Caucasian young lady in the middle of her own personal crisis.

FRIENDS

The doorbell rang as I put the last of the meatballs in the skillet and smothered them with my special tomato sauce. As I wiped my hands and untied my apron, I took a swallow of sweet tea on my way to open the front door. Before I could even get the door all the way open, Lashay dropped a brown bag full of romaine lettuce, cucumbers, and croutons in my arm and pushed a bottle of pink Moscato into my other one as she sped past me towards the bathroom. She threw her umbrella in the stand by the door and her keys on the shelf. She began doing the bunny hop down the hall and ran in place as she unzipped her skinny mom jeans. "Girl, I can't hold it! I really have to go," Lashay said.

I swaddled the bottle of wine under my arm like a football and headed back to the kitchen to keep an eye on the meatballs. I couldn't help but roll my eyes and giggle to myself. As long as I can remember, even when Lashay would visit me in college, she would chug a forty-ounce of beer then wait until the last minute before urgently announcing her bladder was about to burst. It was always an adventure because it didn't matter where she was. When she had to go, she had to go. During our junior year in high school, she came to spend the night with me after a basketball game. I couldn't get the key in the door of my parents' house fast enough. So, Lashay ran and squatted behind the pine tree in our neighbor's yard, next to his yellow petunias. I swear, I saw Mr. James peeping out the window looking down at us with a perverted grin on his face. Another time, she surprised me and came to the homecoming football game while on leave from the Army. It was my second year at the University of Louisville. I had been crowned in the Miss Black U of L Pageant, and while that was exciting, I was happier to see my best friend home for the weekend. Lashay even surprised me and dressed up for the occasion. After hanging out and celebrating my victory, we made our way back to the student dorms.

We were buzzing and having an in-depth conversation about the quarterback making a fifteen-foot conversion on the fifty-yard line. We shimmy-walked in our evening gowns and sashayed in our heels as we made our way through the middle of campus.

Out of nowhere, Lashay paused, "Oh my gosh, Kory, I have to pee! I mean, like I got to go right now!"

I laughed, but I could see the blank stare on her face. "Come on, Shay, we only have a couple of more blocks. You can hold it, can't you?" Nope, of course, she couldn't. Without hesitation, Lashay walked to the side of the building, planted her feet, and lifted the sides of her dress to relieve herself. And what did I do? I'd had a lot to drink, as well, so I figured I might as well go too. I'm sure it was quite a sight to see the pageant queen grasp the tiara off her head and pull down her panties to squat on the side of the student government center to get some relief. Yeah, real ladylike, right? You could hear the splash of golden puddles on the sidewalk. No toilet paper or anything in our possession to wipe off. We just let nature take its course. One of the reasons Lashay and I connected so well, was because we were girlie girls, when necessary, but we were also competitive, tough, and free spirits when we needed to be.

Lashay yelled out. "Thank you, Lord, I almost peed on myself!"

I drunkenly stumbled and attempted to pull myself together, "Girl, the Lord ain't got nothing to do with this."

We pulled our panties up and fixed our dresses. As we turned to walk away, we saw a group of football players standing there staring at us. I grabbed Lashay's arm and pulled her as we half-jogged away. "Way to go, Miss Royal Court!" We heard the team say as they broke out in applause. We were horrified but laughing and giggling with embarrassment all the way to the room.

Some things in our lives have changed over the years, but Lashay's habit of drinking until about to burst has remained the same. Back in the day, we used to drink bottles of Little Kings Beer and cans of Budweiser. Now that Shay is a Christian, her drink of choice has changed. She now guzzles gallons of spring water and sips V-8 Splash with cranberry juice. Don't raise your eyebrows as if to question! It isn't a sin to have a little drink here and there. Lashay just feels it's in her best interest not to indulge. She stopped drinking alcohol when she got out of the Army. I, on the other hand, don't feel the same way. She always brings me my favorite bottle of wine for our monthly girls' night out. Lashay is usually the first to arrive. Camille and Lisa always roll in the door a little bit later. A duo it used to be me and Lashay, but over the years our friendship has now turned into a quartet. Our girls' night out is something that began years ago. It still amazes me the unlikely way I met and bonded with the other girls.

Lashay, with her begging ass, finally wore me down. "Kory, you promised me you would give it a try and go!" Lashay stood with her hands on her hip to make a point.

I exhaled to gather my thoughts because I knew the discussion had potential to go awry. "Shay, I love you like a sister, but I'm not trying to go to a Bible study with all those fake and phony people! My mama used to make me go to church all the time when I was a kid. It's not something I want to do again right now! Now that I'm older, I mean, there are things in my life I need to fix before going back to church. Besides, you know all that I've been through!" I folded my arms and looked at her out the side of my eye.

"Kory, we have all been through things. Stop making excuses! There are some really genuine people there. What's that saying? Don't knock it until you try it. Anyway, Kory, just hush because you promised me, and you are gonna go! There is more to life than just a bunch of drama." Lashay always gives me the mushy 'you deserve better' speech and it always works.

"Ughhh! You get on my nerves. Okay, I will go with you! Just this one time."

That's how I ended up at the Amazing Grace Fellowship Baptist Center Bible Study Group. The gathering of mostly women were welcoming and cordial. I don't really open up to people until I get to know them, but I felt welcome. Lashay introduced me around. We mingled and munched on snacks. We sat in a circle and read a couple of scriptures and then had a group discussion. The only person who made me feel some kind of way was Mrs. Pinchent. I hadn't been to church in years, but Mrs. Pinchent was the embodiment of how people acted at church when I was a kid. She was as stiff as a white dress shirt pressed with starch. She pronounced every word loudly when she spoke. She walked around with her head held high, kind of snooty-like. She smelled of honeysuckle and vanilla when she wisped past me. Her hair was in an updo and her reading glasses sat on the edge of her nose. She looked like a librarian with a Bible clutched under her arm. She would say "Praise the Lord" in between each sentence and she used the phrase more like an adjective than an affirmation. She made me feel really uncomfortable, and when she looked at me, I felt like kneeling and repenting in that moment. There were two other women who specifically caught my attention as soon as they stepped into the room. They were full of laughter and life. They separately greeted everyone with a kiss and a hug. Even though they didn't know me, they greeted me just the same. It was hard to take my eyes off them as they moved through the room. They seemed cheerful and down to earth, not at all the way I thought church people acted. The tall one, Lisa, was dressed in a stylish red dress that showed off the bronze hue of her complexion. She was vibrant and sociable. The other girl was a little shorter and had a cute pixie cut. I don't know what Camille was speaking about, but the crowd around her burst into hysterical, knee-slapping laughter. These women were definitely the life of the Bible study. I saw why Lashay had liked them. As the evening went on, I sat quietly in a corner to observe and take in the interesting group of people. It was obvious that Mrs. Pinchent was rubbing several of the ladies the wrong way. Many would make faces or grimace at the sound of her voice, but no one was disrespectful or rude. At the end of the night, those who wanted to share spoke or said a prayer. Mrs. Pinchent thought she would save the best for last. She stood in the middle of the circle, closed her eyes tightly, and raised her hands as she prayed out loud, "Lord, I pray that these men, but especially these women, Praise the Lord, gathered here tonight will not stay in their worldly ways. I pray they will learn not to bring attention to themselves and distract others from your Word, by wearing red and such. Praise the Lord."

Mrs. Pinchent continued to pray about women in today's society who need direction from God.

I had one eye open as I held Lashay's hand. When looking around the circle, I noticed that Lisa was the only one in the room wearing red. Lisa never flinched while Mrs. Pinchent continued, obviously praying about her. I saw Camille squeeze Lisa's hand, but Lisa never moved. If that had been me, I would have snatched Mrs. Pinchent up! Who did she think she was? She was exactly the reason I didn't want to come to Bible Study in the first place. After Mrs. Pinchent finished, Lisa began to pray out loud. She spoke of where she had come from and the unfortunate upbringing she had as a little girl. Lisa said out loud things no one would feel at ease sharing with strangers. The circle was wiping away tears as she declared her testimony. She gave thanks to the Lord for her journey and the healing she had experienced. Lisa spoke of her strength and her growing faith.

At the end of her prayer, what I will never forget, were the final words she said, "And, Lord, I pray for all the haters in the world, and I shake them off because I know I look good in red." As she opened her eyes, Mrs. Pinchent was glaring at everyone. Mrs. Pinchent clutched the huge black Bible tight to her chest, and without saying a word, she held up her index finger and made her exit. Everyone in the circle laughed from the belly until we cried. We weren't laughing at Mrs. Pinchent but at the way Lisa had turned an emotional moment into a comical one. I learned a valuable lesson that day. Don't judge people, but get to know them for yourself. I had been holding a grudge against organized religion because of a negative experience I had as a child. The timing of this new experience made me open to new friendships. Lisa, Camille, Lashay and I stayed and talked late into the evening. From our deep conversation that night, we discovered we had all faced challenges in our lives. Many women suffer in silence because they don't talk or share their life encounters and life issues. The four of us have been close friends ever since.

As I stirred the meatballs, the sound of Lashay standing next to me rustled me from my thoughts. She was punching buttons on her phone.

"Lisa and Camille just texted they are on the way over, and whatever that is you're stirring and cooking smells great!"

GIRLS' NIGHT OUT... PLUS ONE

Girls' night out was our answer to catching up and keeping abreast of whatever was going on in each other's lives. It was like watching ten episodes of your favorite season on Netflix in one night. The four of us were chatting and talking. This was always how our girls' night out began. We used to see and spend time together on a regular basis but life happened. You know life? Funerals, weddings, divorces, break-ups, make-ups. You know life? Busy schedules, careers, children, husbands, boyfriends and our grand-children. Yes, that's right! We are all now grandmothers and we wear the title of endearment proudly. It's hard to believe we are all in the range of fifty and above. "Black don't crack" and "Fifty is the new thirty." We wear our ages well.

The smell of garlic Texas toast lingered in the living room from the kitchen. Our stomachs panged with hunger as we chatted.

"Is the food ready, because I am starving?" Camille asked.

"Yes, everything is almost done. I will be right back," Kory headed back to the kitchen.

The anticipation of a good meal was building as we could hear the glasses being filled with ice. Lashay was sitting on the couch next to Camille, working on her third helping of cranberry juice. Lisa was standing looking out the window.

Curiosity got the best of Lashay, so she asked, "Lisa, what are you looking at? What's the rain doing outside?"

Lisa set her glass down on the coffee table and proceeded to pull back the sheer panel curtains to take a peek as she explained, "That car has been sitting out front since we got here. And the rain is coming down pretty steadily."

Camille blurted out, "So, what's wrong with that? Maybe it's Kory's neighbor, waiting for the rain to die down before they go into their house."

"Uhm no, I don't think so. A little white girl just got out of the car, looked under the hood, and now she is sitting back in the car," Lisa turned around and raised her eyebrows, "You know, I think there could be something serious going on."

Lashay rose from the couch to get a better glimpse, "Lisa, you really need to lay off the Dateline and 48-hour detective shows. You are always investigating and checking something out."

As Kory walked back into the living room, the group of grandmothers was standing together looking out the window.

"What's going on? What are yaw looking at?" Kory gently pushed and moved between Lashay and Camille to take a look.

Lisa asked, "Is that your neighbor? It looks like she might be having car trouble."

Kory briefly looked and shrugged her shoulders, "No, I've never seen that car before."

Camille pulled away from the group and sat back down, "I pray everything works out for her. Let me know what happens, cause I'm ready to eat."

"Me too!" Lisa chimed in with Camille as she sat and reclaimed the remote control.

"So, are we just gonna leave the lady outside all by herself?" Lashay held up her hands and the grandmothers contemplated what was being asked. Before anyone else could respond, Kory opened the hallway closet to put on a sweatshirt and headed out the front door.

Kory approached the window on the driver's side of the taupe Nissan Maxima. The window appeared to be off track and not aligned vertically. It was obviously stuck halfway down as the cold rain water spit drops onto the passenger inside. The driver was attempting to start the engine, but the engine puttered and wouldn't turn over. The young strawberry-blonde appeared frustrated as she rested her head and her diamond-encrusted fingers on the steering wheel.

As Kory gently tapped on the car window, she heard footsteps behind her as Lashay was catching up with an umbrella. The young woman appeared to be in her late twenties. She could have been a daughter to any of the grandmothers. Strands of blonde curls stuck to the side of her rosy cheeks. Her lips were chapped and shivering from the cold. Her face and green eyes were swollen and tinged with red from crying. She was dressed like money, but the side of her grey slacks and muted chiffon blouse was dark from where the rain water had soaked in. She was a pretty girl even with no makeup, but there was a tinge of blue and purple on her cheek. It looked like the remnants of a bad bruise.

"Hi, I'm Kory, and this is Lashay. It sounds like you're having car trouble. Can we call someone to help you?"

The young lady looked up at the grandmothers as her emerald eyes filled with tears that began to stream down her face.

Between tears and sobs, she began to share her ordeal, "My name is Jessica. I abruptly packed all my belongings as quickly as I could and left. I left my home and my fiancé. I have been through so much. I just couldn't take it anymore. I'm headed back to my hometown in Nashville. I had only been driving about two hours when the car started acting up."

Kory slid her hand through the open window and placed it over Jessica's with concern.

"We are so sorry. Is there someone we can call for you? Nashville is about five more hours down the road?" Kory asked.

Pulling back her hand, Jessica hugged herself with her arms to make heat and shook her head, "No, I mean, I'm just embarrassed and extremely anxious about calling my dad. I don't know what he is going to say. Against his wishes, I moved miles away with a man I barely knew." Jessica continued to share that her fiancé was a prominent doctor who had whisked her off her feet four years ago. He promised to make her his wife and give her a lifestyle different from her humble upbringing back in Tennessee. A handful of broken promises, a broken heart, and a bruised cheek, and Jessica was at a breaking point.

"I just can't believe how blind I was," Jessica held her head down as she expressed disappointment in herself, "Enough of my sad story. My engine light came on and the engine started to jerk and overheat, so I pulled off the highway and ended up in this neighborhood. I probably should call my family, but I'm down to two percent on my phone," Jessica continued to share. Jessica told us she did something she hadn't done in years right before we walked up to her car. She laid her head on the steering wheel and began to pray to God for help. Lashay and I turned around as we both heard footsteps approaching. It was Camille, with Lisa leading the way to investigate what was going on.

"Hey, are you all okay?" Camille smiled to break the ice. Lashay mumbled a quick update of Jessica's story. We looked at each other because we were all on one accord and knew what had to be done.

Lisa spoke softly to Jessica, "Look, honey, you can't sit in this car much longer or you will surely freeze to death!"

Of course, Camille chimed in, "You sure will, and besides, I'm starving."

"Camille!" the grandmothers all said in unison.

Camille changed her tune, "No, what I meant to say is why don't you come in and join us?"

We all shook our heads in agreement.

"Jessica, I live right here, and like they said, we would love for you to come inside. You can charge your phone and warm up," Kory said. I looked at the other grandmothers, and they all simultaneously followed suit.

"Yeah. We know you have to be hungry and tired," Kory added.

Jessica looked at the four women and broke down sobbing. It was the kind of crying that comes from deep within when you can barely catch your breath. We four friends helped Jessica out of the car and huddled around her. We covered her broken self with an umbrella and arms to shield her from the rain. We left the idle vehicle and headed back into the house.

Once inside, we each took a turn to hug Jessica and wipe away her tears. Camille assured her it would be okay, "Baby, it's going to be all right."

After calming down, Jessica sucked up her pride and called her father. She briefed him about her situation.

Relieved, Jessica handed the phone to Kory and continued to wipe away the water from her swollen eyes.

"Hello, no, it's not a problem at all. My friends and I were just getting ready to sit down for a meal. Jessica is our guest and we will keep her company until you get here. Be safe; talk to you soon."

It would be several hours before her ride would arrive. Jessica's brothers and her father would be making the trip to pick her up and carry her the rest of the way back to Nashville. Lashay and Lisa salvaged some warm clothes from my room for Jessica to change into and relax. Jessica was our special guest and now our girls' night out plus one finally began.

Camille was overjoyed when we sat down to bless the food. After dinner, not only did we pour glasses of wine and cups of hot honey-lemon tea, but we poured into Jessica love and understanding. Jessica was delicate and fragile in those moments. She put all her trust into four strangers she had just met. While there were obvious differences between us and our new friend because of our age, race, and backgrounds, we were more alike than not. All we saw in Jessica was where we had been in various seasons in our lives. We had all made mistakes and bad decisions. We knew from experience that after a season of brokenness always comes healing. With age, not only comes wisdom, but a sense of self and the ability to orally re-visit and share trials.

Over the next several hours, we shared with Jessica the uncut versions of our stories of perseverance, without any reservations. We laughed, cried, and described the lessons life had taught us over the years through our upbringing, relationships, and our personal battles.

NOTES:

_____

_____

_____

_____

_____

_____

_____

_____

_____

_____

_____

_____

_____

_____

_____

_____

_____

_____

_____

_____

_____

_____

_____

_____

_____

_____

WHITE PICKET FENCE

Camille

"Jessica, honey, let me shed some light on my life," Camille patted Jessica's leg, "This is so déjà vu! When I was growing up, my mother used to have me sit next to her, just like we are doing right now, and have lectures and discussions with me. Sometimes, reminiscing makes me wince, but it also puts a smile on my face. I smile today because I know how far I've come. I would have never imagined that I would be comfortable sharing my trials and my many mistakes with someone I just met. But here we are. Having this time of discussion with you and the ladies, gives me time to playback what I consider a very pivotal time in my life."

Camille continued her story, "I lay sprawled on the bed looking up at the ceiling. My big pink rollers were hoisted up on the pillow behind my neck. After soaking in a hot bath until my fingertips were wrinkled, I wrapped up in my fluffy robe and slid on my favorite leopard print house shoes. As I lay there, all I could hear were the thoughts in my head and the echoes of my heart beating. And then something else. I thought I heard a faint noise. I froze for a moment as my eyes shifted back and forth. I listened again for the sound. Nothing. It must all be in my head. I got comfortable again and eased back down onto the pillow. Maybe I'm just getting worked up. My girl, Trisha, one of my best friends, is getting married later today. All I have is about five more hours to lay here and relax before the chaos and pandemonium begins. It's not easy putting a wedding together, and it's even more stressful being the Matron-of-Honor. I don't know what I was thinking when I generously offered up my place to be the command center for the bridesmaids to get ready. When Trisha couldn't come up with the funds to reserve the hotel room an additional day, I just stepped up. '*No worries, Trish, we can just all get ready at my place. Let me do this for you!*' Trisha's face instantly lit up with appreciation and relief. Of course, I really didn't have enough room for six bridesmaids, including myself, and two flower girls, not to mention the manicurist, the make-up artist, and the hairdresser. My two-bedroom starter home was going to be maxed out from the living room to the kitchen. I didn't have the room for such a production, but I wouldn't change a thing! I was honored and happy to be supporting my best friend in becoming the next Mrs. Steve Johnson. I heard it again. What is that noise? I kept hearing a sound, but I couldn't pinpoint where it was coming from. Maybe I'm just tired. I have been up since the crack of dawn. As soon as my eyes popped open the second time, I turned on the television to watch the weather forecast. The weatherman said there would be scattered rain showers and then the skies would clear up this afternoon for a beautiful day. The rainwater should be dried up and the sun shining in time for the wedding. Wait a minute. I froze. I hear it again. What is that noise? Raising my elbow off the bed to listen intently again, I hear nothing. Settling back down, paranoia and stress set in. Maybe I need to take this moment to unwind and recap what is about to unfold. A magnitude of thoughts began to cloud my head. The past week leading up to this point had been truly amazing. There was only one issue that continued to resurface in my mind, and other than that, the wedding plans had come together. Trisha's dress was beautiful and her final fitting went well. Of course, I had walked alongside her through the entire process, as her Matron-of-Honor."

"The wedding rehearsal was held the night before in the gym, and it was outstanding. It was a truly beautiful time because all of Trisha's family members and her closest friends were there. I was so excited and happy for her in that moment. At one point during the rehearsal, all the bridesmaids went to the bathroom together. You know how it is with a group of girls. We posted up on the vanity in front of the mirror and giggled and laughed. One of the bridesmaids took out a bag of herbs from her purse and gifted it to Trisha. '*Happy day before your wedding, this will help you relax!*' The bridesmaid handed Trish a bag of herbs. We rolled it up and lit it right there in the ladies' room. We passed it around and took turns indulging. It was thunder! We wanted to stop puffing but just couldn't let it go to waste. I guess I should have stepped in and put my foot down as the head maid and said, '*No, you guys, we shouldn't!*' But I didn't. Remember, I was a work in progress! It must have been some home-grown ganja from the motherland because I could feel the effects instantly. That was the highlight of the wedding rehearsal."

"Knock, Knock, Knock, '*Hey, are you girls okay in there? We are almost finished; we need to practice the processional one last time.*' We all giggled, high and flighty. Trish cleared her throat before answering, '*Yes, Auntie, here we come.'* Trish's aunt was the wedding coordinator, so we didn't want to get caught. We fanned the air around us to clear the smoke, and we got out our last giggles before exiting the bathroom. Trisha hurriedly gave me the baggie with some leftover herb in it. *'Camille, here, keep it. I'm done for the night.'* I gladly took it and hid it in my bra. Weed gives some people the munchies, but it helps me to meditate and think things through on a higher level. That night, after I got home from the rehearsal dinner, I smoked the leftovers Trisha gave me. I was reminiscing and contemplating about my previous relationship. It placed me in a state of why?"

"The same question is popping up in my psyche today. I just can't comprehend how things fell apart with my ex-husband in the first place. And how is it that when I went to get support from my best friend Trisha, I ended up in the arms of her soon-to-be husband, Steve. Why didn't I have full confidence that their marriage will work out? All great questions, Camille! Maybe it's because Steve came to see me last night and we got high together, among other things. Maybe it's because he quickly got dressed and just left this morning before the sun came up. It wasn't until I took my shower this morning, to attempt to wash off the lingering afterglow of our sexcapades. I noticed Steve had left his black alligator belt with the monogrammed buckle that Trisha had given him on Christmas. I didn't want that lying around when the bride-to-be came over to get dressed in my bedroom, so I quickly threw his belt in the back of my closet as far as I could. A half smile formed on my face as I flipped from my stomach to my back to get more comfortable. Here I was, hours before their wedding, and I couldn't even relax. All that pent-up energy was driving me crazy! My erratic thoughts were beginning to stress me out. You know what? I knew what I needed to do. I needed to roll one up, so that I could pull it together. I reached under the nightstand to pull out my herb that was secretly tucked away. As I opened the plastic baggy, the earthy aroma of the leaves and sticks in my stash made my mouth water. I rolled a perfect blunt and lit it up. The smoke made me float, and the influence of the herb allowed me to immerse myself deep into my feelings. As I pulled, inhaled, and puffed, being in a deep, intellectual mode made me smile to myself. Looking up at the ceiling, I recollected that I actually had him first and she was getting my sloppy seconds. But hey, some people say leftovers are better the second day. As the smoke curled around my head and the rigidness in my body turned to Jell-O, I could look back after all these years. I remember when I first dated and went with that fool. I thought I knew him but, boy, was I wrong! It wasn't like I should have. I mean, after all, love at first sight isn't always true. And we were just kids still in high school. Steve, Trisha and I all went to high school together. Steve was two years older. We were sophomores when he graduated and left for college. I had a mad crush on Steve. He was my first kiss and the beginning of my being fast and boy crazy. We would talk on the phone and write each other letters. I was foolish and unrealistic to think this man, who was a successful athlete, was going to go away to college and be faithful to me. He broke my heart in two when I found out he had a steady girlfriend at college. I moved on to the next sexy football player at school. He ended up being my first husband. I married someone I didn't really know. I mean, after all, it was a part of my plan. It was important for me to get out of my parents' house. Living in a house full of rules and religion, isn't easy. Being a pastor's child, especially a pastor's daughter, can weigh heavily on your decision making. I just wanted to be like all the other kids, growing up. All the expectations and the shame if you did something wrong was unbearable at times. I believed in God, but I often felt religion was forced down my throat. I didn't realize it then, but my rebellion would take me down a path that would have heavy consequences. I didn't see the error in my ways. So, I married the first man who proposed to me. Naturally, when I became pregnant, still in high school, marriage was the only option for me. It was important for me to break away from my parents. Getting married, was my underground railroad to freedom and my ticket out. My objective was to get married to the man with whom I was having a child. My goal was for us to get a house of our own and live happily ever after. It had been engraved on my brain that you only have sex with your husband. Thinking about it, makes me shake my head as I look up at the ceiling. I never would have suspected that, after leaving from my parents' house, I would have to grow up quickly and do things by myself. People dream all the time, so why couldn't I? I envisioned my home having rows of green lush grass and a big old dogwood tree that would bloom with opalescent white buds in the spring. My beautiful two-story home would have a porch and a white picket fence surrounding it. I can remember it like it was yesterday."

"Unbeknownst to me, my parents did not like the idea of me dating at the age of fifteen, about to turn sixteen.

My daddy really forbid it, but he thought if he could get ahead of it and keep an eye on me, things would turn out different. When I dated my first husband, my senior year in high school, daddy would look at me and say, '*Camille, something ain't right with that boy.*' I didn't realize that sometimes it takes a man to see in another man, or a boy, who they really are. My inexperienced ass was in love and oblivious to all the red flags. Daddy was upset because his baby girl was on the path to marrying a teenage boy who hadn't figured out what it meant to be a provider or a man. Red flag, we were both young and dumb. Nowadays, folks don't know what they getting into before they tie the knot. Hint, hint, neither does Trish. Sometimes the red flag is not always with the man but can be in the lack of integrity and loyalty of those closest to us. Well, getting back to my story. After graduating from high school, I had already had my daughter and I was working on being a wife and just making it in real life."

"Trisha ended up going to the same college as Steve, down in Bowling Green, Kentucky. Their friendship blossomed and they actually started dating. Yeah, my best friend since elementary school started dating my first love, Steve Johnson. Of course, I gave Trisha the green light. She asked me, '*Camille, are you sure you are okay with it? I would never do anything to jeopardize our friendship.*' I held her hand and looked her in the eyes. '*Trish, we were kids in high school; that's over! I'm marrying the love of my life. I wish you and Steve nothing but the best.*' Best friends, we hugged it out. As my relationship with my future husband got worse and worse, Trisha's thrived. My best friend believed a leopard can change his spots. I've always been told when someone shows you who they are, believe it. I knew my ex-boyfriend, and her future husband was flirtatious and messing around, but I didn't care to tell Trisha. I figured she should have known. Plus, I hadn't always been faithful to my fiancé, either. I did go through with planning my wedding even though the details are just a blur. I was high then too. My best friend, Trish knew I went through, hell, she was in my wedding. My husband and I started our family. We had a place to live for a while. Home Sweet Home. While my first marriage is foggy in my mind, what I do remember so clearly is that my ex-husband became an abusive person. It only took a couple of months after the honeymoon for me to realize something was a little off. My daddy's words had been a premonition I had ignored."

Camille paused and then went on, "Maybe my husband's behavior changed because I confided in him that before we were married, I had also cheated on him. I can tell you that things were never the same after that day. Men can cheat all day long, but when you do it to them, it's a whole different story. I would always tell Trisha everything that transpired. Trisha, what should I do? Should I leave him, or should I stay?"

"Trisha would always say, '*Don't leave him; he's a good man. If it were me, he wouldn't ever have to worry about me wandering off.*' After that, I didn't have to worry about him wandering off because he was too busy trying to hold me to a standard that he was not able or willing to keep. I knew he was unfaithful to me. I would find phone numbers and condoms in his pants pocket when I sorted laundry to wash. He would say, '*Camille, you are my wife, and you will do as I say, not as I do!*' Well, that was the beginning of our first physical fight. A push turned into a shove; a shove turned into a slap. No matter how hard I tried to fight back and get licks in, the strength of a woman is nothing in comparison to that of a man. That was the first real beating I ever took. I felt lost and alone, so after tending to my scratches and bruises, I called my best friend to vent and hear her voice for consoling. She always helped get me through the abuse and my moments of crisis. While my marriage was falling apart, Trisha was newly engaged and planning her wedding. Steve had proposed to her on Valentine's Day. She was so happy and enthusiastic. My house was the first stop she made after receiving her beautiful ring. Of course, she came to show me her ring and to officially ask me if I would be her Matron-of-Honor."

"It would be six months later, that my husband and I had one of the worst fights ever! The slaps had turned into punches. Afterwards, I called my best friend Trish. I slowly placed my finger in the holes of the rotary phone to dial each number and waited to hear her voice. I waited for the line to connect. I heard a voice say, '*Hello, hello.*' Upon hearing the voice, I burst out in a muffled and broken voice. What I didn't know at first was I wasn't talking to Trish, but Steve had answered the phone. '*Camille, Trish isn't here; she won't be back for a while. What is going on?*' Of course, upon hearing the fear and hurt in my voice, Steve came over right away. When I let him in the door, I broke down and crumpled to the floor. Steve angrily looked around the apartment, going from room to room with his fists balled up, looking for my husband. '*Where is he! He wanna fight, let him come pick on somebody his own size*!' As any real man should be, Steve was upset that a man had put his hands on me. Back then, I was petite and a whole one hundred and twenty pounds soaking wet, even after giving birth."

"My daughter was in her crib, crying. After scoping out the whole apartment, Steve picked up my beautiful baby girl and held her close as he got her a bottle to calm her down. My sorry excuse of a husband had hurriedly grabbed a bag with some clothes and rushed out the door when he realized he had blackened my eye and bruised my ribs. Steve, being the real man that he was, laid my daughter back down in her crib. Then he grabbed a wash cloth from the closet and opened the refrigerator to make an ice pack to place on my swollen eye and face. He got on one knee, to bring himself to my level where I had rolled up in a ball on the floor. He was able to sit next to me on the floor, with his back against the wall in the hallway. He pulled me up into his lap while gently embracing me as my body trembled between sobs. Steve gently pressed the ice pack against my face. He whispered, '*Camille, I am so sorry. Girl, what have you got yourself into?*' Eventually, the soothing pressure from the ice compress was replaced with soft kisses from Steve, on my forehead, to my cheeks, and then brushing sweetly on my lips. I hate crying and I hate the pain of that memory." Tears began to fill Camille's eyes as she remembered. "To wipe that remembrance away, I hit and pulled hard. The ripeness of the weed helped to ease the anguish and allowed me to doze off into a comalike sleep."

"I woke up, anxiously realizing, in a couple of hours, I would be walking down the aisle again. This time, as the Matron-of-Honor and not the bride. I wasn't even mad about Trish and Steve getting married. I just didn't want my best friend to find out that I had slept with her fiancé many times, including the night before her wedding, for old times' sake.

Of course, my mama's voice popped into my head. '*Camille, when you get married and become a wife, make it a rule of thumb. Don't let your husband keep company with other women. The second rule of thumb is don't tell other women anything about your marriage.*' Mama used to tell me about fast women being with other women's men. She called them homewreckers. So yes, I guess my mama was giving me a warning about women like me. I guess you can say, I was the original side piece back then.

Jessica, sometimes people are not meant to be. God will send you your true soul-mate or husband in His time. A man will only treat a woman according to how she portrays herself to him. Smoking and getting high and sleeping around does not make the hurt go away. Receiving love starts from within. That's why self-love is so important and necessary."

GRANNY USED TO SAY

Kory

When I think of the rawness of my love for him, it reminds me of some of the old sayings I used to hear from my grandmother. Ray wasn't my first love, and he wouldn't be my last. Who he was to me, was who I needed at the time, or so I thought. Our connection was all feelings and, without a doubt, physical. It was nothing for Ray to come into my presence and all he had to do was look at me. No words were necessary. Uhm… he made my blood boil! I would take him by the hand and we would go wherever our bodies ended up. Leaning against the kitchen cabinet, on the couch, the floor, it didn't matter. He would kiss me, all tongue, and I would melt into his arms like a Snickers bar in the hot summer sun. Many times, the clothes would stay on. Other times, when I was really missing and needing him, our clothes would come off. We did what lovers do. I loved the heat, the sweat, the hardness of his body against mine. I loved his lips and his big ole hands. The roughness and the tenderness, the way he would kiss me all over. Good girl gone bad, I was often the aggressor. Any and every position, like a game of Twister, I welcomed it. There were no expectations and no rules! Just us, being. This was fine with me for now.

In the beginning, my husband was loving and attentive to me. "Kory, I love you so much. I'm not perfect, but the best thing I ever did was settle down and marry you."

I blushed with love and touched my husband's cheek. "Baby, no one is perfect I love you too!" We were a young couple new to this thing called matrimony. Both of us would go to work and come home to build our nest. My husband would come home right after work and help me with chores around the house. We spent family time together. He made it seem like we were in sync and on the same track, building something special. I always told him that two were better than one. Together, I felt like we could survive and make things work. There was only one issue I could think of that could possibly cause problems in our marriage. I had just gotten home from work and a sister was tired. After eight plus hours in the office, I just wanted to sit down and relax for a minute. I took off my work clothes and slipped into some cozy sweatpants. I had a two-hour window before I had to pick the kids up from the after-school program and begin my second shift of cooking and doing homework. No sooner had I sat down on the couch, somebody was pounding on the door. *Bang, Bang, Bang*. I already knew who it was. I got up, frustrated, and snatched the door open. "Look, Lil Larry, stop beating on my door! We just got home from work. You could at least give us time to get home before you come over here!" It's no secret that in black culture if you receive a nickname as a child, it often stays with you through your adulthood. Which is why it was totally insane, when you think about it, that a three-hundred-pound grown man would answer little to anything.

Lil Larry rolled his eyes at me and yelled out so my husband could hear him, "Aye, man, I'll be outside waiting for you." Here we go.

My husband literally skipped down the stairs like a third grader and kissed me on the cheek as he slid past me and out the front door. "Kory, I'm going to hang with the fellows for a bit, love you."

A thorn in my side and a bump in the road were my husband's homies and the company he chose to keep. On a regular basis, his good friends, including Ray, would stop by. They all grew up together in the same neighborhood. Even though they had all been in our wedding, I didn't care for most of them. I simply tolerated them to keep the peace. As my grandmother used to say, *'They didn't have a pot to piss in nare a window to throw it out of.'* They were opportunists, couldn't keep a job, and didn't go to church. I had met my husband in church as a teenager. What I learned much later in life, is that just attending church don't make you right, sanctified, or saved. The more I tried to hang on to my marriage, the more his friends were against me.

One day, I overheard them talking about me while they were visiting my husband, '*Man, she's cute and all, but she takes that wifey thing a little bit too serious. What made you marry her?*'

My husband did not defend me properly. He just laughed it off. They made fun of me and called me church girl and goodie two shoes. It was obvious I wasn't an around-the-way girl and I wasn't from the hood. I was too in love to realize that oil and water just don't mix. My husband's friends encouraged him to party and teased him about being locked up and dragging around a ball and chain. They considered me the heavy weight he was lugging around because he was married to me. I stood there glaring out the front door with my arms folded, pissed! When the fellows came around, I would stay in the house by myself, and I warned my husband? "That's right, you go right on outside and spend time with them because they can't come in this house!"

So, my husband and his so-called boys would stay outside on the porch or in our driveway, being loud and obnoxious. They would listen to music and drink beer. Out of all my husband's friends, there were maybe two I felt comfortable around. Ray was one of them. He was one of the few friends who had a car. Every now and then, Ray would pull up in the driveway in his clean, gold BMW with tinted windows. You always heard him before you saw him because the music was thumping. He was a deep, cocoa-brown color, with curly black hair. I thought to myself, the browner, the better. After all, I used to hear Granny say, "The blacker the berry, the sweeter the juice." More importantly, Ray was kind to me. Even though he recognized I was different than other girls the crew dealt with, he didn't tease me. He made me laugh and smile. He encouraged my husband to nurture our relationship and work on our marriage. I liked him because of that.

One day, Ray stopped by and knocked on the front door like he always did, "Hey, Kory, I didn't want to be rude, I just wanted to say hi and see how you were doing." He put his foot in the door to keep it ajar as I got up off the couch.

"Hi, Ray, I'm good. Thanks for checking on me. Who you got with you?"

Ray signaled for the little girl to get out of the car. When he waved his arm, I got a whiff of his cologne. He always dressed sporty and smelled like he had taken a shower in Drakaar cologne. "Kory, this is Raven, my little girl."

I got down on her level to speak and say hello. She had to be at least eight years old. She was adorable. I really appreciated that Ray took the time and introduced me to his daughter and sister who were piled in the car with him.

Several other times, he stopped by with his girlfriend. Anytime he came by the house, he would knock on the front door and open the screen door just enough to speak to me. Ray would never stay long but just long enough to chat with the fellows for a minute and then he would drive off. He was a couple of years older and more mature than my husband's other friends. They were all street, but Ray seemed to have a sense of family and at least some kind of work ethic. He was like Tommy, on the *Martin Show*. We all knew he had a job, but nobody knew what he did. I never knew exactly where Ray worked or what line of vocation he was in. Deep down in my heart, I suspected. It would be less than a year later that Ray got locked up from hazards of the workplace. He was a street pharmacist. At least twice a month, Ray would call my husband collect from the correctional facility. We would gladly accept the charges to speak with him. Ray was always appreciative that we accepted. He would talk in general, specifically, about the bad choices he had made. He realized he was missing critical years in his daughter's life. He was also sad and depressed because his girlfriend, who was pregnant with his son, decided to leave him. He had not always been faithful to her, and now he had time in lock up to think about it all.

My grandmother's words resounded in my ears, *'Kory, what comes around, goes around.'*

As the weeks rolled past, my husband stopped hanging out as much. He promised me that he was going to change and become a better man. I wanted my marriage to work. I wanted to believe in my husband. We would be on the same page one day, and by the end of the week, he was on edge, trifling, and pushing me to the brink of our next break-up. It wasn't long, before I finally figured it out.

My husband would intentionally pick fights with me, so he could justify being gone and not coming home for two or three days. He would throw in my face, *'Kory, remember what you said? You said you didn't want my friends over here, so I'm going to them.'* This was our routine, pre-Friday argument. Friday was payday. He would disappear after work and come back days later, after he had spent our rent, gas, and grocery money. Liquor, cannabis, and partying became more important to him than our home. The straw that finally broke the camel's back was after we attempted to reconcile one last time. During our last break-up, I got a part-time office job to make ends meet. It got to the point that I couldn't depend on my husband, so I did what I had to do. After working my full-time job, I would pick up my daughter from daycare. Then I would change clothes and drop my daughter off before going to my part-time evening job. Even after we got back together, I didn't quit my second job right away. I had lost faith and trust in my husband. Not to mention, I was three months pregnant. When we fought, the honeymoon stage would always come afterwards, so it was no surprise a baby was on the way. We were down to one vehicle. I would take the car while my husband stayed at home with the kids in the evening. He had a son from a previous relationship and I had a daughter. We did the best we could to make our blended family work. When my mother in-law wasn't available, my husband would look after the kids, feed them, and get them ready for bed. Sometimes on my way to work, I would drop my husband off at Ray's house. He and some of the fellas were getting Ray's house together and making some much-needed repairs. Ray's family had been left with the burden of a rundown house that needed some upkeep. I was proud of my hubby and glad he was finally growing up. I was okay with him doing something productive and selfless instead of hanging around with his friends. Ray had always been so nice to us and he was one of my husband's best friends.

During my sixth month of pregnancy, it came to me while at work one evening. *'I am so tired. This pregnancy is definitely taking a toll on my body.'* My feet were swollen and I was constantly tired from working two jobs. I was moving around like a fat sloth. '*Wait a minute! Why am I working two jobs when I'm married with a husband?*' That was an aha moment for me. '*If anyone should be working two jobs right now, it should be my man. Enough is enough! My husband will need to take the reins and do a little more. He is the man of the house, so he may have to pick up extra hours.*' Without hesitation, I called home during my fifteen-minute break to share my decision with my husband. I was relieved with my decision to quit my job as I headed home. I decided not to worry about money and paying bills anymore. A peace came over me. What I didn't realize, though, was that this was the calm before the storm.

"I know that's right; peace is so important," Lashay stood up and high-fived all the ladies in the room. Jessica smiled from ear to ear as Kory looked at her with a final point.

"If you don't get anything from my story, just remember this one thing. What I've learned over the years, is that when you have peace in the midst of a storm, it means God has not abandoned you but He is walking with you as you go through it."

NOTES:

MARRIAGE TO ME

Lashay

A good thing! I guess that's what I was trying to be when I walked down the aisle of my mother's living room for my first marriage. Or was it at the Little White Chapel, the second time around in Las Vegas? No! I surely got my good thing status right in Nürnberg, Germany when I said I do the third time. You can lower your eyebrows and close your mouth. That's right! I said three times, don't judge me! I don't get married just to have something to do. I take matrimony and vows very seriously. I grew up in a two-parent household, with parents who remained married for over twenty years. In this day and age, that's a miracle. Marriage is something I have always longed for and I even wrote about the topic in my high school Humanities class. Don't mistake what I've said and leave room for thought that everything was as good as gold or smooth as silk in my parents' home. Honey, it was far from that. They had their ups and downs just like any other couple. From a child's perspective, all I could see was love and the fact that my parents were always together. They made decisions about finances and raising children while keeping our household intact. I saw strength and a unified front in my parents' union. On the flip side, I also had plenty of examples of relationships that were weak and fell apart. My Uncle James and Aunt Betty had separate bank accounts, lived together, and slept in different beds. I was only six and I loved sleeping in my canopy bed with pink gingham sheets and my rose chenille bedspread. I just thought Aunt Betty liked having her own bed too. Do you remember how disappointed you were when you found out there was no Santa Claus or the Easter Bunny was fake? Well, that's how I felt when I found out my uncle and auntie were putting on an act for everybody. I came to understand that it was the norm that most married folks sleep together, not apart. I finally got it! Their love had lost its luster over the years and their relationship was more of an arrangement than a marriage. They acted more like roommates than husband and wife.

Then there was my daddy's best friend, Mr. Darnell. He used to sit on the porch and visit. I would always hear him talk to Daddy. '*Look, man, you have a beautiful family. Your wife is lovely and Lashay is as sweet as she can be. But my wife, man, I can't stand her. I'm just in this thing called marriage because it's cheaper to keep her.*' I haven't seen Mr. Darnell in years, but he was right. A divorce can be costly in more ways than one. Despite the things I saw and heard as a little girl, whatever it took when I became an adult, I knew I was going to be somebody's wife. Some kids dream of becoming a fireman or a teacher. I had aspirations of falling in love and being the best wife and mother ever. My husband and I were gonna make sure our marriage worked itself out.

No surprise, at the age of nine, I had no idea what *"working itself"* out meant. I just remember grown-ups throwing the phrase around and Momma and Daddy always working together. *'He who finds a wife finds a good thing...'* That's what it says in the scripture found in Proverbs 18:22. I didn't realize I wasn't the one supposed to be looking, but as a woman, I'm the one who was supposed to be found. Years later, God would reveal to me the true meaning of marriage and love.

The first time I experienced living on my own, I was eighteen years old. After high school, I joined the service to get away. I left behind my family and my best friend. I was going to miss them all, especially Kory. She was going away to college, and even though we did almost everything together, I decided to take a different approach to life. In my eyes, I was grown and mature. I had become a woman. I was caught up in my feelings and I didn't want to follow Mama's rules anymore. So, guess what I did? I joined the United

States Army, only to have to follow the rules and regulations of Uncle Sam, just not my mama's. Even though I lived in a two-parent home, Mama was the butcher, the baker, and the candlestick maker. Daddy worked outside of the home, but my mama ran the home. She was the disciplinarian, the homemaker, and the financial guru. Mama made sure the bills were paid even if she had to rob Peter to pay Paul. Most importantly, she unselfishly gave her whole being to her family. She loved and nurtured her children, to the point of exhaustion. All I knew at the time was I was eager to make my own decisions. I was ready to leave. In my mind, I was grown, and there is nothing more challenging than an internal struggle with two women living under the same roof. There can't be two queens in one castle. I was ready and had no second thoughts about joining the military. That is until I met and experienced Drill Sergeant Paxton for the very first time, in 1984.

In between his barks and yells, the heat of his breath on my face would travel deep into my nostrils, causing nothing but fear to consume my entire body, "Private Crenshaw, we gonna see just how fantastic you are. Just because you a female don't mean I expect any less of you. Do you understand, Private?"

"Yes, Sergeant," I whispered. Drill Sergeant Paxton got so close, I could count the hairs in his nostrils, "I said, do you understand me, Private?"

"Yes, Drill Sergeant Paxton!" I screamed back. My first night in basic training, I cried myself to sleep. Tears became my companion many days following that first encounter. Drill Sergeant Paxton was scary to say the least, but his female version completely surpassed him. Drill Sergeant Faux was her name, but don't let the name fool you. There was absolutely nothing fake about this lady. She could glare you down and call your name all at once, making you question if she was really your mama. She wore that infamous Drill Sergeant black-brimmed hat, with the edges curled up and the string attached, cocked down on her so tight, it seemed as if her eyebrows kept the same expression, whether she was happy, mad, or whatever the mood. Her lips and posture were taut. She had a perfectly rolled bun at the back of her head. Her uniform was creased razor sharp, with lines across her back, and her boots were spit shined so you could see your reflection in them. All jokes aside, this woman was tough. Needless to say, both sergeants prepared me for life as a soldier. I mastered the skills of shooting an M16A1 rifle, throwing a grenade, crawling under barbed wire while the enemy fired, and I conquered the mother of all obstacle courses. I believe both Sergeant Paxton and Sergeant Faux are responsible for my onset issues with OCD. Lord, help! Their painless attention to detail and overt instruction prepared me for life as a soldier. After successfully completing basic training and graduation, I was ready to move to the next phase of my military career. I was moving right up the ladder and my next move was to advanced training, located just across the post at Fort Lee, in Virginia. In six weeks, this is where I would excel and learn the skills needed for my position. I was an Administrative Specialist, aka Military Postal Mail Clerk. I was driven and focused. Nothing was going to stop me from achieving my goals. Nothing, that is until… I saw *him*.

I was waiting in line with my platoon to get some supplies, and another unit was not too far behind. At first, I caught a glimpse of him. I quickly turned the other way when I caught myself staring. The distraction that made me do a double-take and captivated me, was his perfectly aligned, white, flawless teeth. All that white against that chocolate-colored skin made me suck in air. Another look, and I quickly diverted my eyes when I saw him checking me out and giving me the once over. We couldn't mingle with the opposite sex in training. It was a rule in a list of many. No training together, no eating, no sleeping in the same vicinity of the opposite sex. I couldn't talk to him and I was a little shy when it came to first meetings. Intrigued with this man, I would venture out on post hoping to see him. I wasn't a stalker, but I had never seen such an attractive man in all my eighteen years. It was routine, after a week of intense training, to unwind and go out to eat or party. I decided to meet up with some friends from my division to get a bite to eat.

"Excuse me, I'm sorry." I pushed my way through the door of the tiny sports bar that was filled to the max. There was a lot of chatter when I walked through the door and every television was set to the sports event of the night. "Hey, Lashay, over here!" I saw my friends across the room next to the pool table, looking the menu over. My roommate was frantically yelling my name and waving her hands. I smiled and pointed in the direction of the bar as I mouthed, "I'm getting a beer." I decided to take a detour to the bar. The bartender handed me a frosty bottle and as I glanced up.

I saw him. He was posted up next to the pool table with his arms crossed as he waited his turn to shoot. He was laughing and talking with his buddies. '*Okay, Lashay, play it cool,*' I thought to myself. As I walked past the pool table, we made eye contact.

"Hey, Miss Lady, can I talk to you for a minute?"

I nervously giggled and looked around, "Who, me?"

"Yes, you. I'm Trent, and what is your name pretty lady?" He held his hand out to take mine.

"Hi, Trent, I'm Lashay. Nice to meet you." That introduction was the beginning of a friendship that would turn into much more. One day at a time, Trent and I became closer. We began spending time together, and in between training, drills, and platoon expectations, we became inseparable. We spent hours, sometimes days, apart, but once we were able to spend those delicate hours together, we considered ourselves a couple. Throughout the duration of our training, on post at Fort Lee we were destined for a future together. We both understood, being in the Army, there was a possibility we could be stationed at separate posts across the country. Of course, that didn't matter to two people who had fallen madly in love. We were caught up in the moment. We talked on the phone for hours and wrote love letters to each other. I would get misty eyed, as he did, when we were apart. We were in love but too young to understand that time spent together on post was not enough to prepare him to be a husband or me a wife. You know the saying, '*If I had only known then what I know now.*' This was my first serious boyfriend. I wanted to go to the next level. I thought I was ready to be Trent's wife.

After graduation, he returned to his hometown to stay with his parents, because he was a reservist. I returned to stay with my family, because I was on leave before relocating to my duty station. It is not fun being in love and living in two separate states, away from your sweetheart. A long-distance relationship can really tug at the heart strings.

One day after talking on the phone for an eternity, he finally popped the question, "Lashay, Miss Lady, will you do me the honor and marry me?" He didn't get on his knee to ask me in person as I had envisioned since I was a little girl, but I accepted his proposal over the phone, nonetheless.

"Yes, I would love nothing more than to be your wife! Yes, yes, yes!" In a hurry, we planned a wedding and we got married in Mama's living room. One week later, I was on my way to be stationed at a post in Odenton, Maryland. That's right, we got married and moved to two different states. Weeks turned into months and months turned into a year. My dear husband Trent not once came to see or visit me. That's right, I said he neva came to see me! They say distance makes the heart grow fonder, but not in our case. Distance made us grow farther and farther apart. We spoke on the phone and wrote letters, but physically seeing my husband, did not come to pass.

I laid eyes on my husband eighteen months later. I had been ordered to my next duty station at Fort Benjamin. Fort Benjamin was located just Northeast of Indianapolis. I figured I would call my husband to let him know once I got settled in. When I arrived at Fort Benjamin to report in, it was quite a shock to see my husband on post. My heart pattered and began to beat fast when I saw him. I knew that smile a mile away. What turned into excitement, quickly turned into disbelief. What was even more surprising was to find out my husband had a new Miss Lady. A new boo thang! Now I know why he never came to see me. The nerve! You can only imagine the hurt and disappointment I felt! But I was also bothered to the tenth degree! I wanted to choke the breath out of that chick every time I saw her prancing down the hallway of our barracks and drag her ass all over the post. Yea, we lived in the same barracks; it couldn't get any worse. Humph! Who did she think she was? Ole Skank! The game playing and back and forth finally became too much for me to bear. I decided to file for divorce. That's when it hit me. I had never lived with my husband the entire time we were married. How pathetic! "If at first you don't succeed, try, try again." On to husband number two. "I do."

Did God Make Sex Beautiful?

Lisa

It was March 1, 1986. This would become the day that I would never forget, my wedding day.

Walking down the aisle, was one of the longest and most difficult moments of my life. The walk seemed like the *Green Mile*; it felt like an eternity. All I could think about at the time, was the journey I was about to embark on and how am I going to make it work? While my guests smiled and nodded as I walked by, they probably thought I was a beautiful, nervous bride with butterflies. As I dabbed my eyes with handkerchief in hand, they probably thought those were tears of joy running down my cheeks. I was the epitome of a beautiful bride in my Vera Wang knock off with the cream lace bodice and beaded five-foot train. What my guests didn't know, was it took everything in me not to throw the bouquet of cala lilies down, kick off my heels, and sprint back out the church doors. '*How am I going to live this lie? Why am I doing this marriage thing? Surely, by now, everyone knows that I am five months pregnant. I don't love him. This is just a means to get out of the house and away from my mother. I really do want to be happy. No, no, self, you just need to suck it up and do this lie of happily ever after. You can pretend you like having sex. What's that saying? Fake it till you make it. You know how to act, so act like you enjoy having sex with your new husband. The most difficult part of the marriage will be the sex but, girl, you got this. Act it out. Ten more steps, and I will be at the end of the aisle. What am I going to do? I can take a lot of showers and scrub the nasty dirty stuff off that comes with sex. Hold on, Lisa! You are in church, remember Pastor Williams told you in counseling that marriage is a union ordained by God and God made sex beautiful. It's not dirty! It's not nasty! It was created by God for married couples to enjoy. Five more steps, and I will be at the end of the aisle. I need to stop freaking out! I can do this. After all, I have been acting for twenty-one years, my whole life.*' That's a long time in the acting world. With that many years of professional experience as an actress, there would be many awards and accolades received by now.

My acting career began when my Uncle Kenneth would babysit us while Mama was at work. He would send my brother outside to play and lock the door so he couldn't barge in. He used to call me in the living room while watching soap operas on NBC, '*Lisa, come in here and watch the show with me. Come sit right next to me.*' I would shyly walk into the room. And after a couple of seconds of pretending like he was watching television, my uncle would tell me to lie on the floor, and then pull me close to him. Then Uncle Kenneth would start to rub his body against mine while we had our clothes on (*clothes burn me*). Every single day, the same thing would happen, over and over. I didn't really understand what he was doing, except just trying to figure out why this teenager was lying on my six-year-old body. Staring at the television while wishing I was someone else, I never cried. No tears, no emotions, I lay perfectly still, acting as if it were okay, with a straight face.

Oh, yeah, then there was another acting role I had, when Mama's boyfriend was around. When Mama was in the other room or when she stepped out for a while, her boyfriend would creep into my room. While I acted asleep and lay motionless in my bed, he would touch and feel my breasts. I thought if he saw that I was asleep, he would leave me alone. The whole time he was in my room, I would think to myself, *'Doesn't he see the tears streaming down my face? How can he not? Why is he doing this to me?'* I didn't understand. I wanted to tell Mama, but I was unsure what she would say. Should I tell her? Wouldn't she want to know about her boyfriend and how his long nails hurt when he sticks his fingers inside of me? I remember afterwards, I would hold my pee as long as I could until it was unbearable, because the urine would burn from where his nails tore the insides of my flesh. I wanted so badly to tell my mama, but I didn't want her to be mad at me. After all, she talked to her girlfriends all the time about her man and how he would give her his whole paycheck every two weeks. Mama seemed so proud and happy. He would only ask to keep forty dollars to buy whiskey and beer. The remainder of his check, he gave to Mama. Mama wasn't aware, but because of my great acting ability and my not wanting to disappoint her, our household was benefiting financially.

At the age of fourteen, I really learned how to act. I was raped. I was walking home after leaving my friend's house. I took the short cut through the alley. He grabbed me and pulled me behind the garage.

'*Why are you forcing me to have sex with you?*' I asked the neighborhood thug. The pain of penetration as he beat his body against my body, I just remember being hurt everywhere. My legs hurt. My private parts hurt. Why didn't he care that it wouldn't stretch to fit the size of him unless it was torn? Again, I continued acting as though everything was okay. Like it never happened.

Walking down the aisle reminds me of the walk I took home after being raped by a man in the neighborhood. It left me feeling dirty and nasty as fluids dripped from my body, soiling my panties. I didn't feel like I had a choice when that happened. Today, on my wedding day, I don't feel like I have any real other options. Either I have to stay in my mother's house, or I can get married. As I reach the end of the aisle, I think again, '*So, God made sex beautiful?*' As my future husband reaches for my hand and pulls the veil over my head, he stands by my side. I hear the preacher begin to read and perform our vows. I'm there in body, but the thoughts in my head pop to August 3, 1981. It was my seventeenth birthday.

The struggle that I have with sex stems from my childhood occurrences. As I talked with my mother about my boyfriend David, who also had his own apartment, she didn't have any problems with me spending nights with him.

After the long weekend with David, I came home and Mama asked me some questions, "Lisa, how much money does David give you?"

I looked up at Mama, not wanting to get into a debate, "Does he buy you nice things?"

My answer was, "No, ma'am."

My mother firmly put her hands on her hip and told me, "Well, he needs to give you something for your time, Lisa! And if you don't say something to him, then I will do it for you!" What my mama was telling me, in a roundabout way, was I should make it worth my time to have sex with my boyfriend. The sex was okay. I liked it a little bit. *'Thank you for the shoes, and yes, I would love a new outfit, David.'*

At the time, I didn't understand or know that the sexual position I always found myself in was the position I would find myself in life. Beneath someone else or someone laying their weight on top of me. In relationships with men, my feelings, my desires, my purpose in life were always beneath the needs of others. My way of thinking and my direction in life would continue to be a cycle of being in the missionary position.

Today, on my wedding day, I am putting all that aside. I have made the decision to accept his hand in marriage. I am choosing this journey to get out of Mama's house. I will not continue to be beneath others. I will use them, instead of being used.

"What God has joined together, let no man put asunder." Pastor Williams pronounced us husband and wife. My husband lifted my veil to seal our vows and I gladly kissed him back. I can't believe I am a wife!

Fast forward, eight years later. I have two children. I am divorced. Sex with my husband is not an issue anymore because he loves to have sex with men.

YOU DOING TOO MUCH

CAMILLE

'*Whew, that's just what was needed!*' After wiping the slobber from the corner of my mouth, I sat up and swung my legs over the edge of the bed. "There is nothing like a power nap," I said out loud to myself. Raising both arms in the air, I stretched, arching my back, and took in a deep breath through my nose and slowly blew it out through my mouth. The remnants of my high were drifting away but now relaxed and wide awake, my thoughts began to come together.

'*Oh, no, here we go! What is that noise?*' I hear a faint gurgling noise, but I have no idea where it's coming from. I sit still for a couple of seconds, to figure out if I can solve the mystery of the noise. I can't figure it out. I contemplate while I move to grab the whipped mango butter from the dresser and begin to slather and smooth it into my skin. Massaging the concoction into my ashy prone skin zones, I mentally begin to take note of what needs to be done within the next hour. It's 10 a.m. and the girls and glam team will start arriving at noon. Thank goodness it's an evening wedding. We don't have to be at church until five o'clock. I wanted the girls' glam day to have a spa-like feeling. I picked up a vegetable tray and bottled water on the way home last night after rehearsal. Plus, I picked up some chicken wings and chips, because you know a sister had the munchies after smoking. The strawberry Margarita mix is ready and the wine is chilling in the refrigerator. The gift bags for the bridal party are sitting on the kitchen table. The flower vases and the gift from Trisha to give to her groom, Steve, are sitting in the box next to the front door.

Huh! Just thinking about Steve, makes my heart beat fast in one minute with sexy thoughts. The next minute, thinking about him makes me queasy and sick to my stomach. I have tried to stop seeing and thinking about him. On more than one occasion, we both attempted to call off our secret affair, but our chemistry and our connection was too deep. Steve has been not only my friend, but he has helped fill the lonely void in my life. When I heard the tapping on my front door last night after midnight, I already knew who it was. Of course, I should have rolled over and pulled the cover over my head and ignored the knock, but I couldn't. After being high and stressed about my wedding duties, I needed to be with him so he could help me get the monkey off my back. I anxiously pulled the door open.

"Steve, what are you doing here?" I asked, looking up at him sensuously. I placed both of my arms on the door frame, with a stern stance, like the bouncer at the club. Like I wasn't going to let him in, knowing all along I couldn't resist him. Raising my arms to keep Steve out, caused my robe to slightly open, giving him a view of my black satin teddy and freshly shaved legs.

I pleaded, "Steve, we can't keep doing this."

Steve cocked his head to the side as he looked down at me with a slight grin on his face. His eyes went to the opening of my robe and down to my satin-smooth leg. He bent down and kissed me on the lips as he slowly walked me backwards into the house.

Camille paused and then went on with her story, "Again, I pleaded, I don't want to keep doing this. You know this ain't right! Trisha don't deserve this. She's my best friend."

Steve looked down at me and said, "Camille, I know this ain't right. I'm in love with your best friend, my soon-to-be wife. I love her, and I don't want to hurt her. But right now... all I want is to be with you. I promise this will be the last time."

After we got high together, we ended up in the bed for one last romp in the sheets. Oh my God! I don't know why I am having a sense of guilt now about my situation with Steve. Or is it a sense of guilt because I am not doing right by my best friend? Duh, Camille! Trisha has been in your life since we were kids. She is practically like a second daughter to my parents.

Trish shared her engagement news with her family, of course, next on the list, were my parents. She was considerably close with my dad because she lost her biological father when she was a little girl. Naturally, when she asked my father to officiate her wedding at his church, he agreed.

"Camille, come here," Daddy lovingly embraced Trisha, and without hesitation, he said, "I would be honored." I stood next to her, holding her hand, my sister from another mother.

I placed the bottle of shea butter back on the dresser and fell back on my king-sized mattress spread-eagled, like I used to do as a kid making snow angels in the snow. I'm feeling excited about today for my dear friend but, at the same time, a huge amount of guilt. Letting out an audible sigh, while thinking, I felt a drip, and then droplets on my forehead. The wetness ran down my face. As I pushed the weight of my body up on my elbows and simultaneously looked up, I saw a huge form of a wet puddle bulging from the ceiling. No sooner had I said out loud, "Oh my God—." Before I could get the rest of the words out of my mouth, I heard a large pop. After the pop, a flood of water and drywall gushed down from the ceiling onto my mattress, my fresh roller set, and my newly oiled legs. Are you serious? Of all the days to have a burst pipe in my house. That was probably the mystery sound I heard all along. I sat there for what seemed like minutes, in shock that cold water was streaming from the ceiling.

"Oh, Lord!" I held my stomach, sick with despair. "No, no, why today, of all days?"

My daddy had taught me about a lot of things since my husband had left. I learned about changing oil in my car, changing the filter in the furnace, and more importantly where my water shut off was. Jumping up immediately, wiping the water and bits of drywall from my face, I ran to the utility closet to turn the water off. It took me a couple of minutes, and it was harder to turn the valve off than I thought. By the time I got it off, water had covered my bedroom floor and was creeping into the hallway and living room. In that moment, the first thing that popped into my mind was the need to repent and to ask the Lord for forgiveness. After all, this could only be punishment. I mean, I was the pastor's daughter who was sleeping around with her best friend's soon-to-be husband. Now, that's messy! I wasn't proud, but that was my reality.

'Lord, I am sorry! Please forgive me!' There, I'd said it out loud to God. I had confessed. The water from the burst pipe and my salty tears were purifying to my soul. The high from last night was nothing in comparison to this out of body experience. As I continued to look up at the hole in my

ceiling, I finished my confession to God. Next, I got into action. The first person I called was Daddy. When he answered, I said, "Daddy, you will not believe what just happened. I think my pipe burst." Of course, Daddy fussed at me, "Camille, you got your white picket fence, but being a homeowner is a lot of work and it can be very expensive." Mama normally gave the lectures, but now, I was getting it from Daddy. I knew he was right, but this wasn't the time. I was supposed to get the landlord to complete some plumbing work a couple of months earlier, but I postponed it. Daddy kept it up, "Camille, the stress of not getting that problem fixed probably caused the break, with all the rain we had today. When are you going to start listening, Camille?" Through tears, I appealed to my father, "I understand, Daddy, but the girls are supposed to be coming to my place to get ready." Even though I was often disobedient and did not listen to my parents, they have always been there to help me. Daddy stopped fussing when he heard anxiousness in my voice. He agreed that we could arrive at church early to get ready. I got off the phone with him and made several phone calls. I informed everyone of what had happened. Of course, they were appreciative we had a plan B, but a little bummed. The drinks and smoking a little bud while getting ready was now a done deal. There was no way we could pull that off in the church. After cleaning up as much of the water as I could, I hurriedly packed my bags and loaded up the car. I had totally forgotten about the forecast. It had been raining hard, but I didn't realize it. Probably because I was still coming down from last night's high.

So, I arrived at church at the same time as everyone else. Daddy let us in the church and we gathered in the reception hall to set up, as we rotated to get our nails, makeup, and hair done. I felt like I deserved a pat on the back. I was able to mask and hide my shame and guilt while playing my Matron-of-Honor duties to the tee. Right before the wedding was about to begin, Trish and I had a moment to ourselves. She looked absolutely radiant and beautiful. She stood in front of the mirror as I adjusted her veil and fixed her train. She turned around and held my hands. She looked me in my eyes with tears and said, "Camille, thank you for being here for me today. I love you more than you will ever know. I'm so glad that you are sharing this day with me as I marry the love of my life." Of course, I couldn't say anything. I shamefully hugged Trisha back, hoping she didn't see the betrayal in my eyes.

Then, the processional started. I was the last to enter the church before the bride. I walked slowly down the aisle, but all I could see was Steve and how fine he looked in his black tuxedo and red bow tie. I caught his eye, and he held my gaze until he quickly diverted his attention to the back of the church where his bride would make her entrance. The doors opened, and Trisha stood for a couple of seconds before making her way down the aisle. She lovingly looked through the lace veil covering her face towards her future husband.

"And you know what?" Camille sat up straight and asked the grandmothers as they sat and held on to every word of her story. Camille turned to Jessica for a response.

Jessica shook her head and anxiously said, "No, what?"

Camille paused for a second and then dramatically continued. "That good-for-nothing boy had the nerve to break down crying. So much so that his best man had to console him. Between sobs, the whole congregation could hear him whimper, 'Trisha, you are so beautiful. I love you so much.' I stood there in disbelief, thinking in my head, boy you are doing too much. Stop lying! I wanted to cry, but I couldn't because I might not stop. As easy as Steve could turn his feelings on and off, I couldn't. The rest of the ceremony was just a haze to me. I stood there with a smile on my face, but I was numb. After the small reception, everyone gathered on the front steps of the church to send the bride and groom off to the airport to begin their tropical honeymoon. The groomsmen had decorated and tied aluminum cans and streamers to the bumper of the car. The words Just Married were written in big, white letters on the rear back window of the Cadillac. Everyone cheered and threw confetti on the new couple as they walked past."

Camille looked at everyone. Trisha and Steve both hugged their parents and the members of the bridal party. When Trisha got to me, she grabbed me and kissed me on the cheek. *'Love you, Camille, I will see you when I get back.'* She led the way, holding hands as her groom followed. When Steve got to me, he hugged me and whispered in my ear, *'Baby, I hope you are waiting for me when I get back. You look beautiful today.'* I stood there in disbelief but relieved that the man I had fallen in love with acknowledged me on what should have been our wedding day. While Steve and Trisha drove off to gallivant around on a week- long honeymoon, I had to go home and try to figure out how to fix the hole in my ceiling and the hole in my heart.

The grandmothers just sat there, not really knowing what to say. They all just shook their heads. Kory handed Camille the Kleenex box from the table as she dabbed some tears from her eyes.

Lashay finally broke the ice, "Well, damn! Camille, I don't know what to say."

Camille burst out in a nervous laugh. I know, I was a piece of work. I am truly embarrassed and ashamed about how I lied and betrayed my best friend and myself. I didn't love myself back then. It took me years to get over that situation and heal. Healing meant getting to the root of my low self-esteem and improving my self-respect. Jessica, I hope you never experience what I went through. No man is worth a relationship with a best friend, especially if she is close to you like a sister. Men will come and go, but cherish those who are close to you.

NOTES:

TWO WRONGS DON'T MAKE A RIGHT

Kory

"Mommy, Mommy, you're home early."

I opened the front door, and the kids ran to greet and hug me. I was relieved to be home to start the next chapter of my life. I exhaled and gladly embraced them back. "Yes, kiddos, I'm here, and I'm going to be home a lot more often to help you with homework and do fun stuff." As I sat down to spend some time with the kids, they gave me papers to sign and they shared with me how their day went. I asked them about their evening and how they had spent their time, "Did you all have a good day? Where is Daddy?"

"Daddy is in the basement, washing our uniforms for tomorrow. While Daddy sat and talked to the lady in the living room, we sat in the kitchen and did our homework. Yeah, Daddy had company."

"Company?" I asked. They told me about the lady who came to visit Daddy.

"Dad was talking in the living room a long time."

I listened intently while scanning over their student planners and signing off on vocabulary tests, "Well, do you remember the lady's name?"

"No, Mama, we met her before, though."

I thought to myself, *uhm, I wonder who the lady was*. When I asked my husband about it, he brushed it off and told me Ray's sister had stopped by. I thought nothing more of it. She used to ride in the car with Ray when he used to stop by. So, no big deal.

A couple of weeks later, the phone rang around the time I would have normally been at work in the evening. I answered, "Hello."

The voice of a female on the other line asked, "Is this Kory?"

The voice didn't sound familiar, so I replied, "Yes, this is Kory. Who is this please?"

"This is Sherry, Ray's sister. I need to talk to you." Sherry proceeded to tell me that while I was working my second job for the last year, she had been having an affair with my husband. She explained that when I thought I was dropping my husband off to help work on Ray's house, my ignorant ass was delivering him at the front door to be with her. She clarified with boldness and assurance that my husband didn't love or want me. He was hanging around because I was pregnant. As if that weren't enough, the pinnacle and crushing blow was when Sherry blurted out that she had been in my house on several occasions.

"Kory, I was there when your husband washed clothes in the basement. I helped him fold the kids' clothes and we sat at the kitchen table to eat while the kids were playing outside." She informed me that after my husband put our children to sleep, they would make love in the living room and once in my bed. She described to me my home and knew details that only someone who had been deep inside my house could know. I felt sick, hurt, and totally violated. What kind of sick person does this to another, let alone his own wife? It's a miracle that I carried my baby full term. I was a hot mess, dealing with this shit during my pregnancy. After throwing my husband's belongings out on the front lawn, we had our last fight before I kicked him out. It would be many years before I would be able to recover from this level of hurt. What I remember most is the feeling that came over me. I was scared and alone, not knowing what was next, but I was thankful and relieved that I didn't have to deal with the yelling and fighting anymore. I was mad, angry, and hurt, but there is nothing like peace. Peace that allows you to sleep soundly and not have to look over your back.

Finally, one night, the call came. It was a collect call from Ray. Should I accept the call? After all, it was his whore-ass sister who was now coupled up with my punk-ass husband. I accepted. Through tears, I shared with Ray, not leaving any details out, about what happened. This was a deep wound that I could not comprehend. I just kept asking Ray, "Why would another human being take another person through this hurt? If my husband didn't really love me, why did he marry me in the first place? He pursued me!"

Ray listened carefully and told me to pull myself together for the baby's sake. He was sorry that I was going through this ordeal and that he couldn't be there for me, "Kory, you deserve so much more. I'm sorry you are going through this. You really don't know, do you?"

I sat there, perplexed at what I was being asked, "I'm not sure what you mean, Ray?"

"Kory, you really are innocent when it comes to the streets," Ray began to tell me what I hadn't seen. I had been blind in one eye and couldn't see through the other. My husband had graduated from smoking weed to hitting the pipe. I sat and listened with my mouth wide open in disbelief. I felt so stupid. Ray explained about our break-ups and how my husband went missing and spent all our money. He explained my husband's sporadic behavior. I didn't have a clue because I always found fault in myself. My husband having a drug problem never crossed my mind. But who better to explain it to me than a drug dealer? Ray assured me he didn't know about my husband's love affair with his sister. He had spoken with some of the other fellows and that's how he kept up with the latest from lockup. He had also gotten word back to his sister that she deserved an ass whooping for her actions. That's what he said, but Granny always told me, *'Blood is thicker than water.'*

Once my beautiful baby girl arrived, I had to focus on my daughters and attempt to hold it together emotionally. I didn't miss my husband. I was glad he was gone. My baby was six months old when Ray finally got to come home. Initially, Ray would drop by and check on us. He would stop by to talk to me and give me money to help with groceries and baby formula. He even surprised my oldest daughter with a puppy. On occasion, Ray would stop by the house and check on me like he used to. We would sit for hours and just talk. He would also give me a report of how my husband was slipping farther into his addictive and reckless behavior. I thought Ray had changed since he got out and came home. I thought he was doing things differently. Have you heard the saying, *"the only way to get over a man is to get under another?"* Well, that's just what I did. I got all the way up under Ray. I needed his attention and he understood my damage and pain. When I called him, he was right there for me. It's funny how some people grow and others stay stuck. I can hear my granny's voice clearly, *"Kory, two wrongs don't make a right.' and 'Everything that glitters ain't gold."*

Eventually, there was an emptiness for me with my friendship with Ray. I knew it wasn't right and it wasn't the way I wanted to continue my life. Ray was there for me until I desired more from him. I wanted a commitment, a relationship, and hell, who knew, maybe one day I might want to get married again. The same thing that brought Ray and me together is the same thing that broke us apart. Infidelity, deceit, and lies. I found out about the other woman a year later. It was my neighbor who lived two houses down the street from me. Ray hadn't changed at all. I think he really cared for me, but he was stuck in the lifestyle and he loved the streets. I was still numb from the betrayal from my husband, so this just stung a little. The old folks used to say, *"What won't kill you will only make you stronger."* I didn't die, but my heart and ability to trust and love did. Oh, well… on to the next.

SLOW DANCING

Lashay

Funny how the tables turn. Here I was, at my lowest. I'm talking baritone low. I didn't want to be bothered. I was trying to get through the ordeal of being separated from my husband and coping with the idea of my marriage ending in the D word. I wasn't looking for love, but true love ended up finding me again. The thought of getting into another serious thang made me nauseous because I was just getting out of my first marriage. You heard me correctly. I was in the process of getting it done and over with. A divorce is a long process, and mine wasn't finalized yet. For several months, I would go to work, come back to the barracks, and stay confined in my room. Feelings from a break-up can leave you broken and confused. You can be in love one minute, and the next, you can't stand the person. Depressed, I couldn't grasp that my marriage had failed. I was raised to believe that real love and vows taken are supposed to last forever. Look, we had some issues, but I thought it would work itself out like I saw my parents do over the years. I normally dealt with stress by guzzling down cans of beer and E&J brandy. I didn't have my best friend Kory to talk to and I didn't want to worry my mother. Eventually, getting lit, wasted, and tipsy wasn't doing it for me anymore. It gave me headaches and I didn't like that feeling.

My roommate suggested that I get out of the barracks to hang out and have some fun, "Lashay, you can't hide from the world forever. You're being too hard on yourself and it's not good for you to stay cooped up. Go get out and meet some new people. Have you some fun."

I finally took my roommate's advice and went out to get some fresh air. And fun, is exactly what I found. Phillip was tall and had a slender build. Not too skinny, but he had just the right amount of meat on his bones. He was a tall drink of chocolate milk. Not too much chocolate but just enough. His conversation and mannerisms were kind and sweet. They say milk does the body good and that's just what this man did for me. He became a friend, so to speak. Not only was he hot, but he was a soldier. We chatted for hours, and to my surprise, he was interested in hooking up with me. No, I'm not talking about having sex, he wanted the two of us to spend time together so we could get to know one another on a more mature level. After the first date, any uncertainties that I had were gone. I was game! By the second date, Phillip said all the right things, and when I tell you that man was smooth! OMG! He was especially smooth on the dance floor. One weekend, he asked me out and we decided to go to the NCO club on post. The NCO club was for enlisted soldiers and civilians. It was where all the soldiers and locals went to mix and mingle. I got to see and feel for myself just how suave Phillip was on the dance floor.

The DJ slowed things down and started to play *Reason*s by

Earth, Wind, and Fire. You know how the song goes.

> *Reasons, the reasons that we're here*
> *The reasons that we fear*
> *Our feelings a won't disappear, ooh*
> *And after the love game has been played*
> *All our illusions were just a parade*
> *And all the reasons start to fade.*

"C'mon, Lashay, dance with me."

I didn't utter a word. My voice didn't give him the

okay, but the look in my eyes did. When the music started

playing, he gently took my hand and pulled me close. So

close that when I looked up, I could see the rise and fall of

the pulse in the side of his neck. He put his hand in the crook

of my back and pulled me in until my head lay on his rock-

hard chest. I closed my eyes as we swayed and rolled to the

beat of the song. He brushed his soft lips against my neck

and made electricity go through my body. He whispered

sweet nothings in my ear as we savored the lyrics. Right then

and there, I thought about all the reasons I needed him in my

life. When a man holds a woman like that, it can make you

forget a whole lot of everything. Now mind you, I didn't forget I was married, but that slow dance sure helped me feel better about my situation. After several more dates and a few more slow dances, my divorce finally came to an end. In my heart, I was ready to begin a new chapter in my life. I had a glimmer of hope and things were looking good.

We were sitting in the car one evening, just talking about nothing, "Lashay, do you ever think about what your life would be like if you didn't join the Army? Or why things turn out the way they do?"

I loved our little conversations, and as I held his hand, I just laid my head back on the head rest and thought for a minute before I answered, "Yeah, sometimes I do, what about you?"

Phillip tilted his head over to look at me and nodded yes. Then out of nowhere, the question flowed from his mouth, "Lashay, will you marry me?"

My eyes got big and I just sat with my mouth open as I looked at him. Can you believe Phillip asked me to marry him? The last thing I wanted to do was jump right back into another marriage, but here I was again. Although my first marriage didn't work, I wasn't going to allow that to dissuade me from falling in love and marrying again. But I said yes, like a dummy! So now, I was engaged to my fiancé.

Remember, it's funny how the tables can turn. Things can change so quickly. Well, the tables turned again. Something happened that would change the course of my relationship with Phillip. My fiancé had to abruptly leave and go home to Texas to make final arrangements for his mom. His mother got sick and unexpectantly passed away. I never got to meet her. Back home in Texas during his leave, Phillip reconnected with his family and friends. I had to stay behind on post. It was heart-wrenching staying at Fort Benjamin while he was away. The very next week, I received orders and it came time for me to PCS, change duty stations again. The idea of Phillip being at home and me moving to another post made me sick. I decided to initiate plans so that we could travel and spend some time together. I needed to see my fiancé as soon as possible. Being apart from him, made my heart ache and I worried about how he was dealing with the loss of his mother. I wasn't going home to see my own parents and family because I was so in love with this man. We decided to meet and rendezvous for a weekend in Las Vegas and tie the knot. We were so in love and being apart made us want to get married even more. So, I pulled money from my savings account to purchase both sets of rings. We said, "I do," and got married. We stayed in Vegas a few days longer, to honeymoon. Then we reported back to our separate duty stations. I was newly assigned to Fort Sam in Houston Texas. My fiancé was re-assigned to Fort Polk, Louisiana so that he could be closer to his family. I understood completely. As difficult as it was living apart, I kept telling myself we'd eventually be together. I had great separation anxiety because of what happened with my first husband. A couple of weeks after our rushed wedding, things began to fall apart. Death can affect people differently and I believe his mother's death took a lot out of Phillip. He used to give me the sun when nothing but clouds were showing up in my life. They began to fade away. No more slow dancing. The phone calls became less and less. No letters and definitely no visits. "Damn!" This is going down the drain faster than my first marriage. We didn't even get to live together as husband and wife. Boy, I can sure pick them, huh? There is never a problem getting proposed to and getting married. The struggle is staying married. Well, just like my first husband started to remove his attention and found it somewhere else, my second husband is about to get the same treatment from me! My feelings were hurt, but his feelings are getting ready to hurt worse than mine. I met new people at Fort Sam. I started partying hard and going out with some new girls on post. There was an NCO club that I started hitting every weekend. One time, my sorry ass husband finally decided to call on one of my down weekends. I was going through the emotions. I was exhausted and mentally tired of acting out. Our conversation made me feel empty. We mutually agreed that being married long distance wasn't going to work, at all. I had been down this road before. I knew the steps, one by one, that I needed to take to make it as quick and painless as possible. I filed for divorce AGAIN. It was uncontested and my marriage to old Phillip was over in a couple of months. He moved on, and so did I. I know what you are thinking. You probably think, '*Shay can go through them, can't she? She changes husbands like she changes her panties every day.*' Well, you're wrong. Lashay still believes in love and matrimony. She still hopes the right one will find her."

Time passed, and it was time for me to change my duty station one last time. This would be the final move during my Army career. I wanted it to be a memorable one.

Yes, my NEXT husband will have to find me.

MEMORIES OF THE WAY WE WERE

Lisa

The memory of my dad is etched in my mind forever and always takes me back to the summer of 1975. I remember it clearly because that's the year I turned eleven years old. My birthday is in August, and it was a hot, humid summer. My father was coming to meet me for the first time and take me to the state fair and buy me a bicycle. The first ten years of my life, I never thought about having a daddy. But here I am, eleven years old, and realize I have one. During this time, the only example of a man that I had was the one who lived in our house with me, my mother, and brothers. And he didn't even pretend to care about us.

My earliest memories of living with this man are when we lived in a big house on the Parkway. My room was upstairs, in the far corner. I remember one night, I woke up and heard someone crying. I quietly got up from my bed and made my way downstairs to the muffled and disturbing cries. Tiptoeing into the dining room and then through the living room, I stood behind the big arm chair and lifted my head to get a glance. Donald was violently hitting my mom with a leather strap in his hand. The leather strap came down on my mother's backside as she cowered, naked on the floor. Neither one of them knew that I saw what was happening. Or that I was even there. I wanted to help Mama, but I couldn't move. That wasn't the last time my mother took a beating. He was always mean and hitting my mother. One night when Mama was gone, Donald put me and my brother out on the porch. He locked us outside while he called Mama, "Yeah, I'm looking at them now. It looks like it's a little cold out there." Donald had the door cracked just enough so we could hear him, but he wouldn't let us back in the house. "You better be back in this house in twenty minutes or else your children will be sleeping outside tonight."

I yelled to the top of my lungs, "Mama, don't listen to him. Don't come back, stay where you at!" I screamed, hoping Mama could hear me on the other end of the phone, but Donald pushed me to shut me up. My mother came home later that night. Donald eventually let us back in and told us to go to our rooms. When Mama left for work the next morning, she had a black eye. She would wear sunglasses all the time, even when the sun wasn't out.

One day, things got so bad, the police came and put him out, but Mama would always take Donald back. I hated him, but there was nothing I could do. I think Donald is the reason I don't like yellow, good hair-having niggas. They are too pretty, but they behave like ugly people. Donald had a daughter and he treated her like royalty in comparison to how he treated us. He made me feel ugly and unloved. *'Maybe that's why I don't like little yellow girls with pretty hair. They are heifers!'* Donald's daughter's name was Morgan. Morgan was a daddy's girl. Her daddy loved her because she was pretty and she had long hair. Those were the kind of thoughts that would invade my little girl mind, *'It doesn't matter, though, because my daddy is on his way to come and take me on a date for my birthday. He is surely going to make up for all the time we haven't spent together.'* I put on the nicest outfit I could find in my closet and I made sure to comb my hair real pretty. My hair wasn't long like Morgan's, but it was almost to my shoulders. I know because I would pull my hair down and stretch it to see if it had grown. My eyes are big, but I can't do nothin' about that because my mama said Daddy's eyes are big too. I was so excited. I tried my best to be pretty so my daddy would love me and be proud. I need my daddy, even though I don't know him. There was a knock at the door. I stood up straight and tall to greet my father, the way I had rehearsed, over and over. I practiced what I would say to my father once he walked through the door. But as Daddy walked through the door, I just stood there and froze. The biggest tears I could cry came down my face. Eleven years of hope and anxiety of wanting a father and what it meant spilled from my eyes onto the front of my shirt.

Daddy asked Mama, "Why is she crying, what's wrong with her?"

My mother answered, "She does that. Just take her on, she will stop crying in a bit."

I guess my daddy was unnerved by my emotions because he rubbed the palm of his hands on his black pants and said, "Well, I'll come and take her another day." He turned and walked away from me.

I watched the back of him go out the front door. I still couldn't utter any words, but I could feel my heart forming callousness. It caused me to rethink the image of a father figure and what it meant. I decided then and there, at eleven years old, that I would have control over my emotions. I will not allow a man to hit me or make me cry ever again. A man will not walk away from me or hurt me. I will do to them what they have done to me. I will make men cry and I will be the one to walk out on them. I will never let a man have my heart. I will learn to survive in this man's world.

My father returned to see me when I was fourteen, three years later. We had moved and now lived in the housing projects. I heard the doorbell ring, but I took my time going into the living room where my father was waiting. When I came into the room, my father was sitting on the couch with my mother. His arm was wrapped around her shoulder, dangling around her neck. In my mind, I wondered to myself, '*why is mama sitting with the enemy?*'

My friends, Judy and Cindy, came over earlier in the day and were standing next to me. "So that's your daddy, huh?" They stood there with me.

"Yeah, that's him," I had told them my daddy was coming back for me. They came to be nosy and get a glimpse. Like me, they hadn't had a father in their lives and it piqued their interest. There we stood, three teenagers, looking at Daddy like he was an extinct species. As I stood in the doorway and stared, I couldn't comprehend why he was not paying attention to me but was engaged with my mama. I didn't say a word, but my thoughts were full of questions and anger. '*Why is my mother not making him want to talk to me? Why is he not looking at me? Daddy, you said you would be back. Well, you may be too late! My mother has another new boyfriend who beats her. Thomas Jones, Daddy. Look at me. Daddy, please look at me. Daddy, please look at your daughter, your little girl. Can't you see your daughter has been violated? Daddy, can't you see the hurt in my eyes because Mama's boyfriend touches my breasts and puts his fingers inside of me. Daddy, look at me. I am no longer a virgin. My virginity was stripped from me because I was raped. Thomas Jones... Daddy, please help me. Save me, please, from this environment. I have nothing left of me. I don't know who I am. I drink and smoke weed to escape. I am Cinderella, and you are my Prince Charming and I pray that you have come to rescue me. All I do is cook, clean, and babysit my mother's other children. I didn't have them; they are not my children. My brothers seem more like my children, but they are not. She works me all the time. Daddy, please look at me. I am tired. Please save me.'* My mouth never opens to say anything. I walk to the kitchen to get a drink of water to help my dry throat. I had an epiphany at the age of fourteen. My mother and I were fighting for the attention and love from the same man.

After graduating from high school, I temporarily left home to enroll in the Army Reserve. After basic training, I was back home, taking care of the house and my brothers. One morning, as I was cleaning the kitchen, a sheriff knocked at the door. He was serving a summons for my mother to appear in court, regarding child support. I explained to the sheriff who I was and that I was eighteen years old. I shared with him that I was working, taking college classes, and that I was also a member of the United States Army Reserve. He talked to me for a while and explained that we could get back child support even though I was eighteen. When the time came, Mama sent me to court with a letter to give to the judge. I wanted to see my father. I had something to prove to him. The morning of the court date, I dressed up. I wanted my daddy to see that I had grown up and become a pretty young lady. Wearing heels, as I walked the two-mile trek from the housing projects to the Hall of Justice, my feet never hurt. I was focused on making a good impression on my daddy. Besides, I thought my daddy needed to see me. I thought he would be proud of me. Mama told me he had been in the Navy years back. *Daddy, look at me please.* That's all I wanted, was for my daddy to look at me and see me. While in the courtroom, Mr. Thomas Jones, my daddy, did not even look at me one time. When the judge made a decision and ordered him to pay back child support, he glanced and went the other direction as did my heart.

That was a breaking point for me. I so wanted to be loved by a man. I began to act out and go on to sleep with men not realizing I was looking for a Daddy figure. Looking for my daddy to love me. Looking for my daddy to see me as pretty, see me like a yellow girl with long hair. Always yearning to be Daddy's little girl, like Donald Brown's little girl. As I stated before, Mama and I were fighting for the same man. She, too, didn't have a relationship with her father. My mother lived and was raised in a group home, from ages three to thirteen. She recalled and shared with me a one-time visit she had from her father. Her father would continue to have more children. He stopped having children when he reached the twenty-seventh child. Each new woman and new baby would push Mama's relationship with her father farther back down the line. He had less and less time for my mother. My grandmother, as well, did not have a relationship with her father. My grandmother was raised by adoptive parents. Maybe my grandmother lived feeling empty, but at least she had been married four times. My mother never married. I got married, but that didn't end well, either. I realize now that this was a cycle of brokenness.

Today, at the age of fifty-three, I wonder if Mama feels she was dealt a bad hand in life. Sometimes, when I look at Mama lying in the bed at the nursing home, I certainly feel that way about my life at times. I wondered what it would be like to have a man fall in love with me. I believe I would be a princess, and then a queen, in his eyes, growing old together. When he looks at me, I believe he would ponder how did he even get a chance with such a beautiful woman and the mother of his children. That's how I romanticized love and marriage over the years. My prince would protect me from evildoers. He would remind me I am worthy more than I would ever know. He would tell me how special I am and how wonderful life is with me. I would know what kindness and generosity felt like. My prince would make me feel that I am worth him dying for because I am so special to him and I mean everything.

After divorcing my husband, and living in years of pain and hopelessness, it has been my faith that has helped me. I realize now that life is not a fairy tale. I'm so glad I don't look like what I've been through. I have found peace and comfort in a Prince who laid down his life for me and tells me every day, I am His masterpiece. He will take care of all those evil doers. I stopped looking for my worth from my earthly Daddy a long time ago because Christ is my Abba Father. Being adopted by HIM, means he chose me when my father and mother have forsaken me. I'm so happy He chose me. That makes me His princess, and every day when I pray, he answers and sees my pain and says, *'Daddy will take care of it.'*

WHAT YOU DO IT FOR?

CAMILLE

We all continued to talk and tried to get to know Jessica better through conversation. Kory asked curiously, "Jessica, so tell us, did you have any close friends or a serious boyfriend in high school?"

Jessica took a sip of tea and then thought about it for a second before answering. "I had a couple of close friends, but Carson was my one and only real love. He was my first."

Camille pushed her head back on the couch and rolled her eyes. Jessica looked at her and laughed.

"Camille, why are you so dramatic?" Lisa asked as Jessica smiled.

"Go ahead tell us." Kory pulled the pillow into her chest and adjusted her posture because she knew this was going to be some good juicy information. Camille began to share.

"Well, I just have some regrets," Camille stacked two pillows behind her back as she got comfortable. She looked over at Jessica. "When I think about it, I fell in love at least three times in high school, before I got pregnant with my first born. Be proud of yourself that you were disciplined enough to save yourself for your future husband, because as you already know, I didn't."

Kory raised her hand, "Me, either."

Lisa chimed in, "Ditto over here."

All the ladies burst out in laughter.

Camille sat up and took a sip of her tea before continuing, "After the fiasco with Steve and my best friend Trish, I began the healing process. I needed to heal and figure out where my low self-esteem issues really began. Looking back, I think it started when I was a teenager. Maybe it started in high school. I didn't think the most of myself. I have great memories of high school, pep rallies, football games, and school dances. Having friends and changing classes in the crowded hallways in between classes, that was a good time. But the one memory and question that has haunted me for many years is why did I give myself away to someone who didn't deserve it? Or like my mama asked me, *'What you do it for?'* This question pops up in my head every time I think about high school. C'mon now, you know what giving yourself away means!" Camille looked at the ladies as they shook their heads in agreement, "Getting with somebody, doing the nasty, going all the way, or as my parents would say doing what grown folks do. So yeah, I regret that I gave up the coochie, cookies, the punanny. I lost my virginity and gave away what was so precious, to someone who showed me some attention. That was the beginning of my demise for years to come."

She went on to explain, "High school was when everybody was trying to figure out who they were. We all gravitated towards the latest trends or fashions to fit in. My girlfriends and I all wore a scent called Love's Baby Soft and we sported Bonnie Bell lip smackers on a string around our necks. Basically, we walked around in a group thinking we were cute, smelling like baby powder and pouting shiny, pink, strawberry scented gloss on our lips. On Fridays, we would wear our blue jean overalls with one strap hanging off the shoulder and different colored Keds tennis shoes. That was the '*in*' thing back then. Young minded and a little dumb, that's how we acted when it came to some topics. Sex and dating, specifically. I was really naïve. But why was I so naïve? My folks actually informed me about sex. Daddy was obviously uncomfortable with speaking on certain topics, like most men are. He would wave his hand and skittishly say, "Uh, your mama needs to talk to you." Then he would rush out of the room and leave me and Mama alone."

"Camille baby, come here a minute; I need to speak with you," Mama would gently pat the cushion on our cream-colored couch for me to sit next to her. I always knew this was going to be a serious discussion. I knew because Mama never took the plastic off the couch in the front room unless company was coming over. The front room was another name for the living room. Only someone from my generation would understand this. Camille pulled her glasses to the tip of her nose and gave Jessica a wink before continuing.

Everyone laughed as Camille continued her dissertation. Mama discussed the basics with me, about how the female body changes, and my periods. We talked about proper hygiene for a young lady. She also shared that a young lady should keep her legs closed and wait to have relations until she was married, with her husband. Talking about sex with me, her daughter, wasn't easy for her. Mama would often say the word relations instead of the word sex. Whenever she said one of those words during a lecture, she would look from side to side and then lower her voice, lean into me and speak almost in a whisper, '*Camille, if you ever have relations, it needs to be when your married and only with your husband.*' She wouldn't go into deep detail or illustrate what the act of having relations looked like. But Mama, being the educated and classy lady she was, gave me a book to read. The name of the book was Learning about the Birds and the Bees. I guess you are wondering if I read the book? Absolutely not! I had no interest in bugs or animals. That included the birds and the bees. Maybe if they had books about sex when I was growing up like the ones today, I might have read it. My granddaughter's mother gave her a book about the birds and the bees with the Berenstain Bears. I'll bet that is a good read! I feel silly thinking about it now. My friends and I knew the ABCs of sex, but we acted like we didn't. We were just silly acting. My first boyfriend would come see me while my parents went to their Friday night group gathering. Every Friday, like clockwork, my parents left out at six in the evening and returned around nine-thirty. Todd must have loved him some Camille because he rode a good three miles on his Blue Schwinn BMX bike so we could talk and kiss. We never had sex, but he would suck on my neck like a vampire and leave hickeys. If we had an urban dictionary back then, they would be called passion marks. Todd always flew out of the house at nine sharp. He got on his bike that he leaned against the back door of the garage and hightailed it three miles back to his neighborhood. He left right on time, just in case Mama and Daddy got done a little early. Mama brought me a blue hooded bathrobe from JC Penney. That was the style for teenagers back then. Before my parents got back home, I would put my robe on and rub mint flavored toothpaste on my neck where Todd had nibbled. Supposedly, the toothpaste made the passion marks fade quickly. So, when my parents got home, I would be walking around with a hood on, looking like a monk and smelling like minty menthol. My parents just thought I was acting like a normal teenager."

"Then there was this thing where you would reference sex to baseball or kickball terms. If you liked someone or went on a date, everyone would ask what base did you go to? First base meant you kissed. Second base was touching. Third base meant you almost did it and fourth base meant you did the DO! I had only made it to first base. I contributed it to the fact that I didn't consider myself to be the best-looking young lady on earth. I ain't ugly, but I knew there were so many other girls at school who looked way better. Candice, for instance, she was a girl in my third period history class who was built like a brick house. You know, her numbers, her measurements, had to be 36-24-36. She had a Coke bottle figure. Beautiful hair, smooth skin, and a blemish free tone. She could easily have been a model. Her clothes had to have been ordered from one of those upscale department stores. You know the ones you pay a good penny for that no one else seems to have. She was popular and everyone knew her. All the basketball and football players would flirt with her and try to get her attention. Don't get me wrong, I'm not hating on her or anything even close to that. I'm humble enough to admit when another young lady is pretty. People seem to get all caught up in the thought of complimenting someone of the same sex. Not me, though. I have eyes to see and I use them to peep all kinds of things. Anyway, when I compared myself to her, she was a ten and I considered myself a solid six."

All the women were waiting to hear more, so Camille said, "One day, at my locker, I bumped into Jason in the hallway as we were changing classes. Jason was light skinned, with dimples. He wore his hair in a high-top fade. He was one of the best basketball players on the team. I looked up, which was something I rarely did because I was focused on getting my books out of the locker for my next class before the bell rang. "Excuse me. I'm sorry. Camille, right?" Our eyes locked and it was magnetic. I nervously responded, "Yeah, no big deal, I'm sorry, I wasn't paying attention." I was drawn to him and it was so intense, so quick, so wonderful. Jason continued making his way to class, and I went in the opposite direction to mine. Sitting in Civics class, for the entire forty-five minutes, I was giddy inside. Daydreaming, I could not believe he knew my name. He knows who I am. I can't wait to tell Trish and my other friends."

After that incident, I went to school every day with my hair done up real cute. I was looking for an opportunity to bump into Jason again. Sometimes during lunch in the cafeteria, I would see him from afar and stare like there was no tomorrow. I had a huge crush on Jason. He was my first real bad-boy crush. One day, he almost caught me looking but I quickly turned my head and looked in my purse, as if searching for something. My friends and I would talk and giggle about guys all the time, but I never brought up his name. If someone else mentioned Jason, I would say he looks all right, when I knew good and darn well, he made my heart beat faster. He gave me butterflies in my stomach. Not only did Jason play basketball, he ran track and was the quarterback for our football team. Needless to say, he lettered in each one of them. I was book smart and one of the top black students in my Senior class, not sports oriented or anything like it," Camille giggled. The closest I came to sports was being in the Booster Club. If reading a book from beginning to end had been a sport, I would have come in first place every time.

Well, after one of our basketball games, I saw Jason again. After the games, there was always a crowd waiting outside the locker room waiting on the players. It was usually parents, girls who were flunkies, or wanna-be girlfriends, trying to flirt with one of the players. I was there, cleaning off the booster club table. Jason was walking off the court with his head down, feeling defeated. The team had lost to an unranked team by just two points. When I saw him, my heart skipped a beat. Maybe this could be my opportunity to speak with him if only I could get up enough courage. I cleared my throat, "Hey, Jason. You played really well. Good job!" I smiled and sheepishly waved. Jason walked on by for a few steps, then quickly turned around and said to me, "Thanks, Camille." Yep, that's all he said, then he trotted off into the locker room. Two little words is all he gave me. I felt so defeated, because I thought it would at least start a conversation."

Grabbing my purse and my sunken heart, I headed for the exit from the gym to wait for my ride home. Daddy was always punctual and I had a curfew. Standing outside on the curb with my girls, talking about nothing important, I felt a tap on my shoulder. Quickly turning around, I noticed it was Jason looking right in my eyes. We were inches apart and he smelled so freaking good to me. Freshly showered after the game, he smelled like Obsession by Calvin Klein. His eyes were light brown, the kind of eyes you see in light skinned brothers and the sides of his cheeks caved in when he spoke and talked because of the deepness of his dimples. He was almost six foot tall, give or take a few inches, and his smile was so bright. To be a senior in high school, he had a mustache which seemed out of place. He made me smile so hard that my breath caught in my lips before I could respond. It took me a moment to realize that he was actually talking to me. My girls giggled and that snapped me into the present." He said, "Camille, do you think we can exchange numbers?" My inside voice was yelling, *'girl, is this real?'* If so, you'd better act fast and tell this boy yes! I snapped open my purse and grabbed a piece of paper and pen to write my number down. Then I passed it to him and he also wrote down his number and gave it to me. While all of this was going on, we were both oblivious to our friends who had formed a half circle around us. Some were making little comments under their breath, while others were smiling from ear to ear."

Jason turned and walked away while saying, "Later, Camille." All I could do was stand there in awe and smile. I was in LaLa Land until I heard Daddy yelling at me.

He had pulled up beside me with his window rolled down, '*Camille… Camille! Get your butt in this car. What's wrong with you, standing there looking all silly? You know it's almost time for me to be in the bed!*'

It was a week later before Jason finally called me. I wasn't gonna call him first because I was raised to believe you don't chase boys. Only fast tailed girls do that. His voice was deep, even deeper than in person. We talked for a couple of minutes the first few times, but then it got to where we were talking at least an hour or two every day.

"Camille, why ain't you got no boyfriend?" he asked. I answered shyly, "I don't know, I just don't." The real reason was because my parents were strict, but I didn't want to get into all of that. We decided it was time to meet for our official first date. Of course, I had a curfew and I had to make my parents aware of my every move. Answering the questions correctly, the who, what, when, where and why, would determine if I could go or not. There were no cell phones or texting back then, just a good old-fashioned watch. Daddy tapped his wrist with his finger before I walked out the door, 'Camille, be back by curfew. Not a minute past.'

I kissed Daddy on the cheek and responded with a, 'Yes, sir.' I closed the door behind myself and saw my parents watching from the front door as we pulled off.

"Our first date was a movie and dinner, which consisted of a hamburger, fries, and a drink from the nearest McDonald's. It was a Friday night and no school to worry about the next day. Jason had borrowed his dad's 1983 black Cutlass Supreme. It was coal black, with shiny rims, and black interior leather seats. It smelled like a mixture of leather, sandalwood, and tobacco. It smelled masculine and manly. In the middle of the movie, Jason leaned over and whispered into my ear, '*Do you want to leave and ride down by the river for a few minutes?*' I, of course, said, 'Yeah, sure, let's go. As long as I don't break my curfew.' Not thinking anything strange and not wanting to go home yet, I agreed. We held hands on the drive down River Road to get to the park. When we arrived, Jason pulled in on the side of the river where cars usually park for a good view. It was a beautiful night. It wasn't pitch dark, because of the light from the stars and the lighting off in the distance. It felt so romantic. You could see the rolls of the waves on the murky Ohio river and a barge passing by in the distance. Talking and talking, like there was nothing to do and nowhere else to be, Jason grabbed my hand and pulled me close to him. Placing a kiss on my forehead, then moving down my face to my cheeks and kissing each one, he finally landed on my lips. I had practiced kissing on my pillow and talked about French kissing with the girls, but this was different. Remember, I had barely been to first base. Tongues twirling and doing acrobatics, our kiss was long and passionate. Continuing to kiss me, I now believe Jason knew all the right questions to ask. *'Baby, can we move to the back seat so we can have more room to hold each other? You know my legs are kind of long.'* Once again, I agreed, because I was stuck on stupid. Obsessing over details that did not matter. 'Yes, of course,' my mouth said, but my immature mind was in heaven because he called me baby. Not even opening the doors, we climbed over the seat. You know once we got in the back seat, there was more going on than just holding each other. *'Cammy, I've been wanting to hold you and spend time with you for a minute.'* He convinced me that he had been checking me out for a long time and that it wasn't a coincidence that we locked eyes that day in the hallway. In between our kisses and caresses, one piece of clothing came off at a time. Being gullible, I was in a trance and going along with the program, so to speak. My body was betraying me with every kiss and every touch. My heart pitter pattered and my mind was on lockdown. I got a little nervous as I slid my pants off but kept my panties on. If you sit on leather too long, you can get a little hot and the texture of the material can chafe your skin. Jason laid me down and began making his move to do what grown folks do. All I could do was move the way he wanted me to move. '*Yeah, Camille, put your leg right there.*' The windows were fogging up and the leather against my butt didn't feel too good. I was afraid but willing. My mind unlocked and I thought this was wrong, but my body kept going like this was what it wanted. It was over before I knew it, and he hurriedly moved away from me. Let me repeat… it was over before I knew it. Now, I know it should have lasted a lot longer, but you live and you learn. I was in shock but, for some reason, pleased because Jason chose me. I thought to myself, Camille, get it together, fix your clothes, straighten your hair and act like everything is all right. We climbed back into the front seat, he started the car and took me home. The ride home was okay. He did continue to hold my hand and kissed my forehead. There weren't a lot of words spoken between the two of us. When we pulled up to my house, of course, Daddy had left the porch light on. I got out of the car and as I exited, Jason looked at me and said, '*Later, Camille.*' I watched him pull out and drive back down the street. Oh yeah, I made it home five minutes before curfew."

Camille sighed, took a sip of tea and then said, "One day turned into two, and three turned into four. We saw each other every day at school and he never said another word to me. I would look at him in the distance with his friends and think to myself, Camille, what a fool you were, to give yourself to him. My self-esteem and self-worth were nonexistent after that incident. I am often still conflicted and confused as to why it took me so long to value myself. Even though I had parents in my life to intervene and explain life situations in a mediocre fashion, I didn't listen. They laid out a roadmap for me to be a high achieving and successful young lady. I just couldn't see it. My daughter arrived about six months after I graduated from high school. When she was about a month old, Mama called me into the living room to sit next to her. Mama stretched out her hands to take her granddaughter from me and hold her close. Mama looked at my baby lovingly and then glanced back at me angrily and asked, "Camille, if you ask yourself what you do it for? Or if you ask yourself, what would you have done differently, do you know the answer?" Looking and thinking back now, my inside voice probably should have told her, '*What I would have done differently was read that damn book you gave me and listen to what you told me.*' But I respectfully looked up at Mama and said, "Yes, ma'am." Then Mama said, "Camille, having this baby is not the end of the world; children are a blessing." I heard her but quickly tuned her out. I was mentally and physically tired from having little to no sleep. Taking care of a newborn was harder than I thought. What I know now is that I mistook being in love for the act of sex—two totally different things. And, I got caught up in the church talk of getting married and having a husband. My focus should have been on meeting the right person God sent for me. Not just the first person who came my way and said nice things and made me feel warm and fuzzy inside. Some people get it, and others don't. A lot of people, like myself, seek things or people who will superficially fill a void. Giving our bodies and minds away, in the end, does more damage to our psyche, emotions, and our spiritual well- being. Your worth can only come from the Lord."

NOTES:

MY COUNTRY MEMORIES

Kory

During my season of abstinence and taking a break from men, I had a lot of time to be by myself. Angry, I would cuss. Sad, I would cry and pray. My children, family and friends, made me feel alive, but when alone, I often contemplated and wondered why things turned out the way they did. Am I not deserving of love and happiness? Or do people just use and take advantage of you to get what they want? I started to meditate and think about where I had gone wrong. Scrutinizing the past, I tried to remember if something happened to me when I was a kid. But all I have are great memories.

My fondest childhood memories revolve around humble, rich lessons of family, and growing up during a period when life was simple. During this time in the early

1970s, there were no cell phones, cable television, or the latest technology gadgets. Life was unpretentious. As a little girl, I was spoiled but loved. My parents were working class and I spent plenty of time with my grandparents while they were at work. Mama worked third shift and attended nursing school. Daddy worked a full-time job during the day. My grandfather was also a provider. He would go off to work early in the morning and be gone all day while my grandmother took care of me. I would arrive at their house before my grandfather left for work.

"Hey, baby girl, let's have our time before I leave."

"Okay, Grandaddy," I followed him through the house, his little shadow. I had no idea of what my grandfather did for a living. I just remember he would faithfully get up and get dressed each day. He would wear work shoes and a checkered flannel shirt. There was always a pen in his front pocket. He would boil a pot of water on the stove and then scoop two large, heaping spoonsful of Sanka instant coffee into his mug. He would do the same in my ceramic white coffee cup. At five years old, I would sit and drink black coffee with my granddaddy before he left to make ends meet. *'Lots of sugar and no cream please Grandaddy.'* That's the way we started the day.

My grandmother was disabled and lost her leg because she had the sugar. What I learned much later in life, was my grandmother was a diabetic. She lost her leg due to the complication of the disease. Her leg was amputated from the knee down. Unlike the prosthetics of today, made of alloy and titanium, she rose early in the morning to put a sock over her stump and strap on her wooden leg. She would use a cane or a walker to get around. Before she put her clothes on, she would take a needle syringe and inject insulin into her stomach. Even though she was disabled, I didn't see her that way. I didn't see the limitations she had because of her illness. She got around and took care of me just fine. Grandma didn't drive, but a lot of women in her generation didn't drive, either. The love I had for my grandma was great. She loved me and I, her. She spent time with me and provided for me the best that she could. She had experience. After all, before I was born, she used to take care of other people's homes and families like other maids did. When I came along, the first grandchild, Daddy encouraged Grandma to do for me, to do for our family, what she had done for many white folks. So, she became my fulltime caregiver, teacher, and a homemaker. Of course, I didn't understand the great undertaking or the blessing it was to stay home and be raised by my grandma. Being reared by my grandmother meant all food was prepared and cooked by her hands. There was no such thing as fast food. I grew up eating carefully planned home-cooked meals from scratch, three times a day. Breakfast was often eggs, ham, or bacon with toast and fruit preserves. Oatmeal came out of a carton with the face of a Quaker man with a blue hat on the front and was made with milk and brown sugar. My favorite breakfast staple was white rice with butter, white sugar, and a slice of cinnamon toast. Sometimes, I would have a bowl of Cream of Wheat. Remember the story of Goldilocks and the three bears? Well, I think Goldilocks was eating Cream of Wheat, not porridge. I can only imagine that porridge looks and tastes the same. The only thing instant that I was exposed to was Tang. Every morning, I would drink a glass of the orange drink mix so I could be like the astronauts. After breakfast, I helped my grandmother wash the dishes and clear the table to prepare for lunch. After lunch, we would clear the table to prepare to make dinner. We had a schedule and followed the routine of cooking and cleaning to the tee. Lunch and dinner were well-balanced meals of home-grown vegetables, fresh fruits, and homemade breads. My favorite made from scratch signature desserts was brown sugar and lemon pie. Grandma would whip them up on a whim. The pies were always topped with homemade meringue. I would pull up the wooden stool so that I could look down into the bowl. Grandma would crack eggs and add sugar and cream of tartar to create a frothy white concoction that would stiffen. She would bake the pies until the snow-capped meringue turned a golden brown. Sometimes, she would make butter cake too. A pinch here, a dash there. My grandmother didn't follow directions from a cookbook. She mastered the recipes and had all the information in her head, like all great cooks do. My favorite part of baking was that I got to lick the batter from the spoon and bowl. Funny, nowadays, they say you can get salmonella from eating the raw eggs in batter. I don't believe it, though. We did it and still living to tell about it today. While we waited for the pies and cakes to bake, we would wash dishes in hot, soapy water that smelled like fresh lemon detergent. In those minutes, I had to be quiet as a mouse so I wouldn't make the cake fall. If I forgot and skipped through the kitchen too many times, I'd have to go outside and fetch a switch to help me remember to keep still. On occasion, if I got to close to the stove and burned myself, Grandmother would pinch off a piece of burn plant and place it on my skin to let the ooze ease the pain away. I was grown and an adult before I realized a burn plant was aloe vera. My days were filled with the time I spent with my grandmother. I never sat idle or got bored. When I wasn't helping Grandma cook, I would have some down time. Leisure time for me was playing in my grandmother's Coty powder and putting rouge on my lips and cheeks. She was fair-skinned and I would emulate what I saw her do when she would dress up. I would play in her jewelry and my ears would turn red and hurt from the clipped earrings that would leave an imprint on my earlobes. Other times, I would flip through and look at pictures in her McCall and Good Housekeeping books.

My favorite magazine, though, was the itty-bitty Jet that the mailman would bring. I loved looking at the pictures of brown girls who looked just like me. Out loud, I thought, "When I grow up one day, I am going to be the beauty of the week." The same time every day, we would watch and listen to my grandma's favorite soap opera, *As the World Turns*. We would listen to the drama of the soaps while we finished our household chores. I learned to smooth wrinkles from the bedspread with the palm of my hand, to make a perfect bed.

"Kory, go to the other side and smooth it out."

"Okay, Grandma," The goose down pillows were fluffed to perfection.

Other days, I would help wash the cabinets and the baseboards down. It was easier for me to stoop down and dip the cloth in the hot, bleached water. If I did a good job for the week, Grandma would give me a silver dollar. When the weather was nice, we would sit outside on the porch and watch life go by on Cedar Street. Grandmother would sit on the iron porch glider and I would sit on the steps. I would watch and learn from her as she gave me instructions. Sitting on the porch, she taught me how to cut and core apples, shuck corn, and snap green beans. "Kory, be careful with that knife, take your time. And don't pinch off too much of the bean, just snap the ends!"

"Okay, Grandma," We would make small talk and laugh in between taking sips of fresh-squeezed lemonade. Sometimes, we would eat fresh grapes or ice-cold slices of melon while we enjoyed the fresh air. A big cigar tree sat on the sidewalk, and a huge rose bush decorated the front gate. I loved to smell the roses. Gently pulling the bud to my nose, I would take a whiff without a thorn pricking my little fingers. The smell reminds me of a lotion my grandmother would wear called Rose Milk. Sometimes, I would pluck flowers from the honeysuckle vine, pulling the stem from the yellow flower, and let the nectar drops brush my lips as I tasted the sweetness.

Every summer, I would go with my grandparents to the country. Granddaddy would take us on a week-long trip to visit my great-grandmother who lived in Tennessee. My grandfather would load up and stuff the back of the pewter green station wagon. I would sit in the back between the boxes and the suitcase. There was a blanket sprawled on the back seat with a pillow, where I would doze in and out of consciousness as we made the journey. The smell of fried chicken and fresh baked rolls would envelop the car. After driving many miles, we would stop at a rest stop to stretch our legs. My grandfather would park near a picnic table so my grandmother wouldn't have to walk far. She would unwrap a red and white checkered napkin off top of a basket filled with good smelling food. I would smash the dough of the bread in between my greasy fingers and pinch off a piece to chase with bits of meat from my drumstick. Our bellies full, we would get back in the car to finish our travels. I would look out the window to take in the pleasant scenery of pastures and green along the way.

My great-grandmother's house was an old white wood structure nestled in a hollow. A rustic, weathered barn and tree-covered hills sat behind the house. I remember waking up to the distant cry of roosters every morning. Peering out the screen door, I would see a white, foggy haze hovering over the fields and a dewy mist on the grass. After breakfast, I put on my clothes and hurriedly ventured outside with my Uncle Johnny. He always wore overalls and a checkered shirt. He was up early, slopping the pigs or getting on his tractor to tend to the cows. I had everything to do but nothing to do. I loved being in the kitchen with my grandmothers to watch the country way of cooking. They would soak beans in a mix of saltwater and cut a chicken up and dip it in egg wash. I would sit with both hands on my cheeks and watch as each side would brown and pop in a Crisco-covered black iron skillet. If I sat there long enough, I got to be the official taster to let them know if more sugar or pickle needed to be added to their recipes for just the right taste. My favorite meal was Cole slaw, corn pudding, and fried fish. There were always greens, tomatoes, cucumbers and red onions in a vinaigrette and sugar dressing. When I wasn't in the kitchen, I would run and play outside. I would take a stick and make creations in the red Tennessee clay. On occasion, I would get chased by a guinea hen. I was hardheaded and did not heed the warning not to get too close. The guinea hens were temperamental and territorial. My grandmothers and grandfather laughed heartily as I would get too close and then run for my life as the black and white speckled bird chased me around the yard. Sometimes, the sky would gray and cloud up. Back then, there was no weather radar doppler system. My grandmothers always knew when rain was coming. They knew how the breeze would turn or they would hold their nose to the sky and say, *'I smell rain coming.'*

It was nothing for a downpour to flow from the heavens, and I found joy in running through mud puddles and playing in God's water park. After the cool of the rain, the heat would come. Heat and humidity were high, to the point you didn't sweat. You were just sticky wet. I love and miss my simple country memories. I remember, we would sit on the porch in the evenings and Granddaddy would make homemade vanilla ice cream. Cream, sugar, vanilla, and dry ice. We would churn the wooden ice cream maker by hand until the vanilla goodness was finished.

Dirt roads and barbed wire fences between me and the brown cows. I was tomboyish and I would try to tag along and keep up with the men. One day, I went with my granddaddy and uncle to watch them butcher a goat to prepare the meat. It was a way of life to live off the land. Going into the dark shed up the road, my grandfather pushed open the creaky wooden door. I saw a goat hanging by its feet, split down the middle of its stomach, with blood dripping into a bucket. It looked disgusting. I remember the flies and the smell of hot goat's blood. I don't eat goat meat to this day. Despite this memory from the country, I loved to run around all day. By the evening, my heels would be black from going barefoot, and the remnants of the day's meals would decorate the front of my shirt. I was a dirty, hot mess. There were no street lights, so when it got dark and the daylight was gone, it was pitch midnight dark outside. In the darkness, you could see the flicker of lights from the lightning bugs. In the country, it would be so quiet that it was loud. There was no plumbing or running water inside the house. My grandmother would pour water in a metal pan and give me a good wash down with Ivory or castile soap.

As I got older, I no longer enjoyed going to the country. I got all citified and sidity, used to indoor plumbing and the luxury of central air. After the deaths of my grandparents, the trips to the country faded to none. I got caught up in the day-to-day life of working and the hustle and bustle of our generation. It wasn't until the birth of my youngest daughter and the discovery of her high functioning autism that memories of my grandmother's disability began to come back to me. My grandmother loved and lived hard, despite her condition. Despite the challenges and hardships that life gave her. Though times have been difficult raising my daughters and dealing with my heart damage, I'm still healing. I'm just now grasping and understanding that some of my husband's demons were a result of him not having a sound mind. Mental illness and addiction were not topics discussed when I was growing up. I have researched and found sometimes it's a blend of genes and hereditary junk from both sides. In the case of my daughter, it is a powerful cocktail because she is already showing signs and traits of her dad's illness times ten. When I became an adult, and even when attending church, mental illness was always something that happened to that family or those people over there. If it was an issue for anyone, it was usually a family secret kept quiet. That's how black folks cope with the topic.

"Church, let's keep that family lifted up in prayer as they go through their storm, amen."

"Amen, Pastor."

It infuriates me that we will promote taking blood pressure medicine so we won't have a stroke. We will eat the hell out of brown beans and greens to stay healthy so we won't clog our arteries and have heart disease. But when it comes to sickness of the mind, such as bi-polar disorder or depression, we are quick to tell an individual, "Baby, just read your scripture and pray every day so you can become more spiritually mature." I know that prayer is always good and necessary, but so much more is needed. Sometimes, the paths we take in life and how we survive is a great reflection of our childhood experience and sometimes, it is not. As I continue to contemplate, I have had no choice but to take a step back and slow down.

"Kory, stop having a pity party! Sometimes, bad things just happen to good people."

How we grow up and the seeds that are planted within us, can mold and shape our being. I can only think that the love and energy poured into me as a child, is what has kept me from totally giving up on others. Life has thrown me one curve after another, first with my husband, and now especially, with my daughter's illness. Curve. Medication changes. Curve. Endless psychiatric visits. Big curve. People judging my situation. What people don't realize is that a child with a disability of the mind grows up to be an adult with a disability of the mind. They deserve love and understanding without being judged, the same as anyone. Each day, I pray for discernment and wisdom to push through. I have felt alone over the years, but I'm grateful for the genuine friendships I have formed. In spite of challenges, each day, I have found peace and comfort in enjoying the simple things in life. It often brings me back to the country memories of my childhood. Just the thought of trying to figure it all out, can be overwhelming. When life gets stressful, sometimes I just sit on the veranda and inhale, to breathe in the fresh air. Here I am, still a little girl at heart. I yearn for the peace and serenity of the country. Every now and then, without even thinking about it, I take off my shoes

and go barefoot.

LOOKING BACK

Lashay

'Okay, Lashay, snap out of it, you are not that little girl anymore.' All of a sudden, it seemed like all eyes were on me. "What? Did I miss something?"

"Where did you just take a trip to?" they all joked and asked, including Jessica. I realized that I must have been out of the loop for a while, so I put my best foot forward and decided to travel back down memory lane and let Jessica know what the others have known for some time. You see, I explain to her about the different forms of control and how it can hold you hostage physically, mentally, and spiritually. One person's experience with abuse is not always the same for the next person, but the scars are always present. Whether you can see them with the naked eye, or see it through one's actions or thought process. However, it happens, it's wrong, and when we're old enough to realize it, we can make a conscious decision to let go and let God. Looking back, is hard sometimes, but it is also good, to see if you've made any progress. I had to question myself about what role I played in the failure of two marriages. Maybe things in my past had something to do with my pursuit of love. I stopped listening to the girls in Kory's living room and went deep inside my mind, only to find myself looking at this little five-year old girl. Her innocence was so sweet and pure, she trusted everyone who came into contact with her. Just feelings of sickness, with no words to match. I snapped back to reality for a quick moment, just as Camille was handing me a bottle of water. But as quickly as I snapped back, I was gone again. I remember the words he spoke to me, "Let's go upstairs."

"Let's go upstairs, you guys, I want to tell you something. You boys stay down here. We will be right back in a little bit." These are words that have continued to haunt my mind ever since I was little. Our neighbor, who lived down the street, would often babysit us. He was a teenager, but Momma and Daddy thought he was responsible. They trusted him to watch us. He would take me by the hand, and my two little girl cousins would follow behind to go upstairs. Our rented house was nice and roomy, with extra bedrooms upstairs. Why do I remember it was rented, and why do I remember it wasn't ours? It's amazing to me, the little, intricate things a five-year-old mind can recall. I remember it like it was yesterday. We would lie on the bed, and he would take his wiener out and ask us to touch it. My cousins and I would take turns. He would want us to put it in our mouths, and try to sweet talk and coax us into it. I wouldn't give in to this request because it was just ugly. I knew what we were doing was bad. He would touch us and lick between our legs. When it was happening, I felt as if this couldn't be real and pondered, *'when is Mama coming home? I don't want this to be happening to me.'* One day, I heard a noise downstairs. *Who is that? I wondered. It sounds like Daddy.* The four of us fixed our clothes and hurried down the stairs.

Daddy questioned the babysitter and then us. "What were you all doing up there? There is not really any reason for anybody to go up there."

If I recall correctly, I said the first thing that came to my mind and fell off my lips. "We were looking for a toy."

It doesn't end right there. Later on, Daddy is standing in the mirror in the bathroom checking his hair. He asks me again, "Shay-Shay, tell me again why were you all upstairs when I came home."

I tell him the truth this time, "Daddy, he asks us to go upstairs so we can play house."

Daddy asks me, "Shay, how do you play house?"

I told Daddy, "We are the mommies, and he acts like he is the daddy." I was only five, but I knew that playing house like that was wrong. I wanted Daddy to go and confront him or beat him up, but it never happened. I remember Daddy calmly leaving after checking his hair and clothes, to go back to work. He must have told Mama because when she came home that evening, she asked if the babysitter had hurt me. I told her no, but really, I can't even fathom the hurt that I carry from the experience as a five-year-old innocent child. I don't think he ever babysat for us again, but the damage was done. Do I think it ruined my thoughts or perception of sex? No, not really, but I know that it definitely made me feel like I was a bad little girl. How could this be? I was only five, I didn't know any better. I naturally trusted the older person who was put in charge, to watch and protect me. The reason I feel like I was bad is because I carried the shame inside silently for over forty years before I ever told anyone about it.

'She is so cute, and look how nice she looks in her clothes. Your hair looks really good. Did you do it yourself?'

I would politely respond and say, "Thank you, thank you." It would come spilling out of my mouth, but that's completely the opposite of how I felt inside. Have you ever wondered why you question someone's intent when they give you compliments about your looks or how you do things? Or where they think you're going in life? In all fairness, it has absolutely nothing to do with them. It's all about how you see yourself. When I look back at my childhood, I was pretty shy.

I was that kid who clung to their parent whenever being introduced. Or I would cautiously peep in a room where my cousins were playing, wondering if it was okay for me to join in with them. Questions were probably in my mind back then. *'Why don't they ask me to play? Am I not good enough? My mama combs my hair every day. Well, my daddy brushes over it and sometimes changes my ribbons and my outfits. I brush my teeth and wash my face. So, what's the problem? I'm fun to play with and I like to laugh a lot, but really, I'm sad inside.'*

Here's the kicker, I have never talked to my mother about it since the day it happened. Why? Because, I don't think Mama can handle talking about it because of things that happened in her own life. It was MINE and I don't want her to take this on as hers. So, it's to protect her, not me. I am now free, not only because this person has since died, and I must say that I was not sad about it at all. But I can speak that it happened with the understanding that it was not my fault. I doubt it can ever be erased from my memory, but I know that it doesn't have a hold over me anymore. It was at that moment, when I looked directly at Jessica and realized she was really understanding the impact of her fiancé's control. She couldn't speak, but the tears in her eyes spoke for her. All I could do was open my arms as she fell directly into them. We both cried, I mean one of those gut-wrenching, snot-coming-out-your-nose sobs. And no more tears could be formed. We let go and became quiet for what seemed like an eternity.

NOTES:

WHAT IN THE WORLD

Lisa

Just imagine coming home from a long day at work, to find your three-year old son running around the house unsupervised. Then, only to open your bedroom door, to find a man lying on your bed watching your husband model newly purchased bikini underwear. That day, would be the beginning of many situations I would find myself in, only to say, '*What in the world?*' There have been many times I look back to see, were there any clues of my husband's homosexual activities? Guys hang out; that's what they do. So, it wasn't out of the ordinary that my husband's friend, Blake, would come over. His wife didn't have a problem with him being at our house for football night. "Lisa, we are going into the den to watch the game, is that okay? We don't want to keep you up." I did not mind at all, "Okay, that's fine, just don't have the television up too loud."

My husband was always recording music, watching sports, and movies with his guy friends. It was a hobby. I didn't think anything else about it. In hindsight, I believe they may have been in the den having sex under my very nose. I now wonder if the same men whom I welcomed into my home as his friends, were also sleeping in my bed? The way a person treats you, lets you know how they feel about you. Like most relationships, we didn't start off with problems. He was very kind to me and somewhat protective. One evening, he asked, "Lisa, did you call your mother to let her know you're spending the night at my place."

I sarcastically replied, "Why would I do that? My mother doesn't care."

Montez called my mother himself, because he didn't want her to worry. I'm unable to recall exactly when the change began, but my husband began to treat me differently.

We had fights and arguments, but our problems were deeper than that. I remember standing on the bus stop and watching my husband drive past. No regrets of leaving me standing there, he did not give me a ride to work. We lived in the suburbs outside of the county, but I worked downtown in the city. A car ride was only twenty minutes, but the bus ride one way was an hour and a half. I was eight months pregnant, on my way to the bus stop after work, when I thought my water broke. I frantically called my husband so he could come get me. "Montez, I think it's time, my water broke."

There was a long pause. "Lisa, just get on the next bus, you'll be all right. What do you want me to do about it?"

I didn't question my husband; I just did what he told me. He didn't come, but when I finally made it home, there stood Manning. Manning was another one of his *'friends.'* Manning and I once got into an argument and I told him that I would mop the floor up with him. He turned to run out the door, and believe it or not, my husband ran after him. Again, I say, *'What in the world?'* Nowadays, they say, *'What the hell!'*

Montez began to hit me, but I would hit him back. One incident, my son had a neighbor friend over to watch a movie. Montez and I started arguing and he put me in a headlock while I was holding my baby daughter. Needless to say, the little boy told his parents what he had witnessed while at our house. His father talked to my husband about putting his hands on women. In spite of their conversation, we still had physical altercations. Montez would also make comments about my looks. He said to me one time, "Lisa, your nose and lips are big, why did you cut your hair?"

I said, "Your MAMA!"

It was like he was trying to break me down or break my spirit. What he didn't know, was I was used to abuse, but I was also a fighter.

In the midst of all this turmoil, of course, a major concern was what if I am HIV positive or catch AIDS? In the '80s, AIDS was a big issue. Sexual orientation was not talked about or embraced openly during these years. Many people did not make known their sexual preferences. Homosexuals were condemned, and many lived a double life out of fear of not being accepted or harmed. I was in the military, so we were tested annually for AIDS. I tested negative every test, but it weighed heavily on my mind for many years. Although he and I were divorced, the diagnosis and ramifications of the disease may not have shown up for years. There was no cure or medicine back then. My other major concern was my children being embarrassed because of their father's sexuality. Most of the neighborhood knew about their dad. The humiliation came from me thinking people were questioning how I didn't know.

After our divorce, one day, my ex-husband's friend knocked on my door. He proceeded to tell me that he and my ex were having sex. He was looking for an ally to side with him against my ex-husband. You see, he found out where I lived because he was with my ex when he dropped off our children. As I listened, I became more and more angry about the situation.

"The nerve of you, to come to my house and tell me all of this mess. The next time you knock on my door, trust me when I tell you I will cut your ass! Don't you ever let me see your face around me or my children again!"

And do you know, I never saw that bastard again. Once, when I went to pick my children up from visiting their dad, there was a man laid up in his bed while my kids were in the house. Montez came outside, and we got into an argument. After hitting him with my fists, he knocked me down. I began hitting him with a rubber workman's dummy hammer I got out of the car. My daughter would later find pictures of her father naked and lying in the bed with other men surrounding him. My children became hurt and angry.

My daughter blamed me for many years for the divorce. It was Spiritual Warfare, but at the time, I didn't recognize it or know.

"Jessica, stay woke. Listen to your inner you. Guard your heart and your mind. Follow your heart with your mind. There is a reason God tells us to guard our heart and our mind. Never just follow your heart. Remember, the decisions you make today will have a lifetime effect on you and your family. Yes, I'm still fighting in this battle. However, I have come to learn, the battle is not mine; it's the Lord's. I am no longer angry or feel shame. I talk to my ex-husband and text him almost every day. God has kept me as I continue to look to Him for my help."

NOTES:

_____

_____

_____

_____

_____

_____

_____

_____

_____

_____

_____

_____

_____

_____

_____

_____

_____

_____

_____

_____

_____

_____

_____

_____

MISSING MY MOTHER

Jessica

Jessica attentively sat and listened to the grandmothers' stories of how they overcame and conquered the giants in their lives. She was present in flesh, but the women could tell her mind was far away.

Lashay asked, concerned, "Jessica, are you okay?"

She gave a faint nod of her head. The awkward moment came to an abrupt end when the jingle from Jessica's phone made everybody jump. We were all on edge and a little skittish after Jessica's fiancé started to binge call and text her, trying to figure out her whereabouts. It got to be so bad, the grandmothers suggested she block her fiancé's number because she was becoming increasingly upset. "Uh oh, it's probably my dad." Jessica hurriedly untucked her feet from beneath herself and leapt up from the couch to take the call. We were all sleepy and giddy with girlfriend silliness. After our delicious pasta dinner, we had gotten lost in the passing hours, talking and sharing. It had been a rollercoaster of emotions, from laughing and sobbing. Everyone welcomed the sudden interruption. It was like intermission at a play on Broadway. Everybody took time to get up and stretch. Camille and Lisa scrolled through their phones to check messages and the latest posts on social media. Lashay ran to the bathroom, while Kory went to the kitchen to refill glasses. Then, as if someone had blinked the lights signaling the show was about to start the next scene, we met back in the living room to pick up where we left off. We had started dinner about six, and it was already after eleven.

Lisa did a double take as everybody came back into the living room. "I can't believe we've been talking for over four hours. Where did the time go?"

Camille's eyes got big. "Y'all know it's past my bedtime."

We were all chattering and laughing when Jessica was the last person to return to the room. The grandmothers hastily stopped talking and looked up at Jessica with anticipation to hear the latest and greatest about her family and the status of their arrival.

"What's wrong, Jessica?" Lashay looked up at Jessica with concern."

Her eyes were filling up with tears and she quickly wiped them before they began to descend down her face. "No, it was a good call. I forgot I was supposed to call Mrs. Robinson to tell her I was safe."

"Mrs. Robinson, who is that?" Lisa implored.

Jessica fanned her face with her hands to dry the tears.

Lashay whispered to Kory, "What's wrong with that child, something else is going on? She is so emotional; I hope she is going to be okay.

Jessica composed herself. "Let me just start from the beginning."

Memories of my mother's cancer are pieced together in a foggy patchwork of recollections in the back of my mind. I was only six years old when the terrible disease took a toll on my mother and took her life. I thought it was as simple as dealing with allergies or a sore throat that you get in the winter time. Can you imagine being a little girl and watching someone you love fade and wither away? My mother was so sick. I can't remember all the medical terms and treatments. All I remember is hearing words like terminal, chemo, and stage four.

"Jess baby, can you go in the family room with your brothers and watch television?"

"Yes, Momma," I grabbed my Barbie and skipped into the other room.

"Mommy just needs a minute to rest. I'm so tired." My mother was alive and strong one day and weak and suffering the next. Her funeral was held a month later.

I loved my mom so much. Over the years, the memories of the way she smelled, the sound of her voice, and how she looked began to fade. What didn't disappear, was the yearning and ache in my heart for my mother and how much I missed and needed her. My dad and brothers did the best they could to raise me and shield me from harm. They would comb my hair into pigtails and have tea parties with me. It wasn't easy being the only girl in a household of four men. As much as they tried to protect and love me, there was still an emptiness and a void that I couldn't explain. Fortunate for me, I still had female influences from my Aunt Sheila and both sets of grandmothers. They would pluck me away to bond during shopping trips and baking projects.

Everyone tried so hard, but what I missed from not having my mother around, I sought out in other ways.

At the age of twelve, I rebelled and started hanging around the wrong crowd in school. I remember getting caught smoking cigarettes behind the bleachers in gym class. Probably doesn't seem like a big deal, but I was attending the same private Christian school my dad and brothers had also attended. It was our family legacy and a tradition amongst all siblings to excel academically. When Sister Marie called my father from the headmaster's office to tell him to come and pick me up immediately, I knew I was in big trouble!

"Mr. Johnson, this is Sister Marie. I need to discuss a situation with you."

I was sitting in the chair in the office when she called my dad. "You can call my father; I'm not sorry or remorseful for what I did. As a matter of fact, I will do it again!"

Sister Marie looked at me over the top of her glasses, stunned. I just remember being angry. A hard force field like shell was what I developed to keep the hurt out. I was mad at the world! My brothers and dad were beside themselves and didn't know what to do with me anymore.

"Jessica, what is wrong with you, why are you lashing out?"

I would reply, "Whatever, it's my life! I can do what I want!"

We used to go to church and spend time as a family. Our ski-trips and vacations to the beach used to be something I looked forward to. But now, that didn't matter anymore. A temperamental teenage girl going through puberty, the men in my life didn't know how to handle me. My brothers would whisper and tiptoe around me. "It must be that time of the month." I was obsessed with going to nursing school to become a nurse, like Mom. Before her passing, she would talk about how God had given her a love for others. She treasured being a nurse and took special interest in every patient she cared for. I idolized Mom and wanted to follow in her footsteps. Upon graduating from high school, I changed my mind. Just like that, I no longer wanted to go to college. My family was dumbfounded. I ended up getting a job at a local diner, as a waitress. It was less than what I was capable of and not what I truly desired to do in my heart. In retrospect, I believe I was depressed.

I was in the diner working a double shift, when I met Carson. He was a doctor in town for a medical convention. He was so handsome. I knew he was much older than I was, but I didn't think our conversation would lead to anything. When we started talking, he totally caught my attention. Even though he knew I was much younger than he was, he still took an interest in me. He made me feel grown-up and beautiful. We exchanged numbers and began talking and texting on the phone every other day. When my father and brothers found out that I was seeing someone, they were happy for me. That is, until they found out Carson was fifteen years my senior. I had just turned nineteen and he was thirty-four. My brothers were not having it. They were ready to break Carson's neck. They tried to explain that a man his age had no business being with me.

"Jessica, he is too old for you. There has to be something wrong with a grown man who wants to be with a nineteen-year-old. You have your whole life ahead of you!"

"So, something is wrong with him because he sees something in me? Stop babying me!" With clenched fists, I stormed to my room and slammed the door. I threw myself on the bed and cried convulsively. I would pick apart their advice and take it personally. *'If mom were here, she would understand.'*

To no avail, my Aunt Sheila tried to talk to me as well. One day in late fall, we were on our way to the outlet mall to shop for boots. It's something I looked forward to doing when my mother was alive. The trip turned sour quite quickly. "Jess, I talked to your dad and we are both concerned about your relationship with Carson."

'Oh, great, catch me off guard to talk to me, when my only escape is to jump out of the car in the middle of nowhere on the expressway,' I thought as I rolled my eyes.

"Jessica, I know what it's like to be young and in love, but I think it might be best if you date someone closer to your age. Think about it, why would a thirty-four-year-old man want to be with someone your age?" She waited for a reply from me.

All I had for Aunt Sheila was the cold shoulder. I didn't have any words for the remainder of our trip. I had heard it all before, from my brothers. She really made me hornet's nest angry when she questioned Carson's maturity and purpose. I thought about it all right and flung my hair as I interpreted her words. Was she insinuating that I wasn't pretty or smart enough for Carson and me to be together? I didn't care what my family thought. I didn't want to hear what they had to say. I know Carson really cared about me and loved me. He promised to take care of me and told me he would give me a life I deserved.

Dad's hurt was obvious, I could see it in his blue eyes, "Jessica, I love you, you will always be my little girl. Even though I don't agree with you, I will support whatever decision you make."

I listened to dad intently as my eyes filled up with tears. I was an adult, so he couldn't make me stop seeing Carson. I was extremely surprised when Carson proposed with a 14-carat emerald cut diamond. Of course, that helped me make my decision. I began to pack up my belongings, and I moved three states over, to live with my future husband.

The home I moved into was a beautiful, five-bedroom ranch that sat in the back of a cul de sac, in a gated community. Carson was divorced, and the house was more than enough room for just the two of us. He had two children, but his ex-wife had full custody. He explained that he loved his children and didn't want to put them through an unnecessary custody battle. I believed everything he told me. I didn't have children of my own and I didn't have any idea what questions to ask. Questions like, "Carson why don't you ever spend time with your kids? Why don't they ever come to visit and spend time with you? When will I get to meet them?"

Everything was great and lived up to my expectations. I didn't want for anything. Carson told me I didn't have to work. In the future, he would be okay with me working or even taking some college courses. But right now, he wanted me to stay at home. I was okay with that. I would stay at home while he worked his shifts at the hospital. He gave me an allowance and wrote down a list of chores that I had to complete before he got home. I wasn't allowed to leave the house until he returned home, and no one, absolutely no one, could come inside the house. I thought the rules were a little strange, but I was okay with the arrangements. Days turned into months, and then I began to get bored and tired of staying inside. The newness and excitement began to wear off. Things began to spiral downward one evening when Carson pulled into the driveway after work. I was outside pulling weeds in the front yard. It was early summer, and the weather was gorgeous. I had completed my chores and was tired of being cooped up. I decided to go outside. I put on a cotton tank top and khaki shorts. The warm sun felt good on my skin and fresh air was exhilarating. I didn't think it was a big deal, especially since I was just in the front yard. Not to mention, I had the phone with me in case Carson called. The next-door neighbor had finished mowing the yard and he, along with his wife, came over to introduce themselves to me just as Carson pulled into the driveway. Carson came over and shook Mr. Robinson's hand. We laughed for a minute. They were a little older but seemed like a nice couple. Carson pulled me close and kissed me on the forehead as we said our goodbyes. After conversing and laughing with the neighbors, Carson firmly held me around my waist, kissed me on the lips, and walked me inside the front door to the kitchen.

I was so excited that he was home, "Honey, don't you think the yard looks much better?" I proudly pulled the gardening gloves from my hands. It was my first time weeding and tilling alone.

Carson responded by back handing me in my mouth and punching me in the side with his clenched fist, "Didn't I tell you not to go outside! You should not go outside until I get home. Jessica, don't ever do that again!"

I fell to the floor, stunned and shocked. I felt blood trickle from my lip as I lay against the refrigerator. This would be the beginning of a volatile and controlling relationship and the first of many incidents that left me black and blue. I had never in my nineteen years experienced such humiliation and confusion.

Every time Carson put his hands on me, he would come back and apologize, "Jess, I'm so sorry, baby, please forgive me. I will never hurt you again."

I would silently cry, and like a wounded sheep, I would lay my head on his shoulder and take him back. He would shower me with gifts and promise this would be the last time. He was sorry that he lost his temper. He blamed his temper on what his ex-wife had put him through. And every time, I took him back because I believed him. One day when Carson went to work, Mrs. Robinson came over. She had a package in her hand that the mailman had accidently put in her box. We began to talk, and one thing led to another. She told me that she was quite surprised to find out Carson was in another relationship this soon after the incident with his ex-wife. She shared that she was the one who had to call the police and the paramedics while her husband pulled Carson off his wife after he exploded in the front yard. He was upset with his wife because she didn't follow his rules. Mrs. Robinson could tell from the look in my eyes that this was news to me and I was terrified, "Jessica, you need to be careful and take care of yourself. If you ever need anything, please call me or come over anytime." She hugged me, and from that day forward, she became my confidant and friend when Carson wasn't home. I was too scared to leave the house, so we would rendezvous on the screened porch in the back or sometimes in my kitchen. Our backyards faced one another. She would enter the back gate and come over to keep me company. She was much older and wiser than I. She reminded me of my mom. I can only imagine that if Mom were alive, we would have similar conversations and talks.

One day, Carson came home early between shifts, and my chores weren't completed. He hurt me pretty bad that day. I knew that I couldn't take it anymore. On more than one occasion, I picked up the phone to call Dad but hung up before the call went through. I was too embarrassed and afraid of what Dad would say. I should have listened to my family. I felt like I deserved what was happening to me because I didn't heed their warnings. Finally, one day, I was so sad and lonely in the house. I went to Mrs. Robinson's house.

She quickly brought me in. I was crying so hard. She wiped away my tears and then she got up from the sofa. She came back and placed car keys in my hand. "Jessica, I already talked to my husband about this because I knew this day would come. When I moved in with my husband several years ago, all I brought with me were the clothes on my back and that old, banged up Maxima that's in the garage. We keep the oil changed and gas in it. The window is messed up, but it runs good enough to get you home.

Mrs. Robinson placed the keys in my hand, "Take it, it's yours. I think it's best that you go home to get away from this situation." I hugged Mrs. Robinson as tightly as I could.

Mrs. Robinson hugged me back and brushed my hair lovingly with her fingers, "Jessica, it's not safe and you deserve so much more. I knew something was going on with Carson and his ex-wife, but I just kept my mouth shut. I didn't want to be the nosy, intrusive neighbor. I often prayed to God and asked him to forgive me for not calling the police or going to check on her sooner. If I had, things might have turned out a lot different for her. Thank God for second chances."

Mrs. Robinson held my hand and made me promise to let her know when I made it back home safe to Tennessee. I ran back to the house to pack and get as much as I could in the car before I left for the long drive home.

FULL CIRCLE

We sat quietly and listened as Jessica finished her story. Our hearts hurt at the thought of a daughter losing her mother so young.

"Ladies, I have laughed and cried so much, my jaws are tired, and my eyes are swollen."

Nodding our heads in agreement, everyone sat quietly and took in the moment. We had all experienced loss and hurt. Jessica's phone rang again, interrupting the awkward silence.

"Uh oh, it's my dad, I bet he is almost here," Jessica hurriedly untucked her feet from beneath herself again and jumped up and answered her phone. While she was out of the room, we all got up and stretched like newborn babies waking up from a nap. Lashay proceeded to go to the bathroom, one of her favorite places. Camille and Lisa went to raid the kitchen for more pasta and hidden snacks in Kory's cabinet. Minutes later, we naturally gravitated back into the living room. Jessica came back with tears in her eyes.

"Baby, are you okay?" Jessica knew we were inquisitive and gave an answer before we could inquire any further.

"Sorry, I'm so emotional. It was good to hear my dad's voice. I'm anxious because I have some news to share with my dad and brothers."

"Mhh mhh, I think I already know," Lashay nodded her head with confidence.

Jessica softly touched her belly and spoke in a whispered voice, "I'm almost three months."

"What in God's green earth! Three months?" Camille yelled out and fell back on the couch like she had a fainting spell. Jessica began to sob even harder.

"Jessica no, you have every right to be emotional," Kory calmly held her hand and asked, "Does Carson know about the baby?"

Jessica cried harder, "He doesn't know because I haven't decided whether or not I'm going to have this baby. But now, after hearing your stories, I'm undecided. I'm having second thoughts."

Lisa exclaimed, "Praise the Lord! You don't know the plans or purpose that God has for your baby. Just like Mary was not aware of the depth and significance of her child, but trust me, it's all for a purpose. Even your dreams of being married to someone you love who returns that love, can still happen."

Lashay chimed in, "And I'm sure your dad would love for you to continue your mother's legacy, by becoming a nurse," Lashay slid past Camille and playfully popped her on her leg so she could come back to life.

"Jessica, you did say Carson was a doctor, well, that's some good money. Child support and college tuition."

"Won't HE do it!" Camille jumped up from the couch as the grandmothers clapped their hands with laughter. Jessica was reassured to know her situation could still be all right. Kory looked at the clock and realized Jessica's family would be arriving soon. She began clearing the table and running water in the kitchen for the dirty dishes.

Camille, quickly grabbed her purse and jacket, "Well Jessica, it was so nice to meet you." She reached out to Jessica and gave her a long hug.

Lisa twisted her lips and looked at Camille, "Camille why is it that you always suddenly have to leave when it's time to do some work? Like washing dishes or setting the dinner table."

Camille continued to put her jacket on, "Lisa you all have kept me up late, now I got to get ready for bed."

Jessica held on to Camille's arm hoping for a final explanation, "But wait, we have a couple of more minutes, I want to know what happened? I mean, Kory, after the baby was born did you get back into another relationship? Lashay, what happened after your second marriage? Did you get married again? I have so many questions. And Lisa, I can't believe the secret your husband kept! Camille, did you ever tell Trisha the truth about Steve?"

Camille uttered, "Well, I guess you were taking it all in after all." Everyone laughed.

Before walking out the door, Camille lovingly embraced Jessica one last time as the other grandmothers nodded with approval, "Jessica, I guess, those answers will come in another story at a different time if the Lord chooses. Be safe."

The girl's night out was coming to an official end.

"Bye Camille, text us when you get home to let us know you made it," Lisa yelled out the door.

Camille waved as she got in her car and drove away. Just as Camille pulled off, headlights flooded through the window.

"I bet that's your family pulling up now," Kory stated.

Jessica made her way to each of the remaining grandmothers. "I was thinking we had maybe put you on overload with so much information in such a little time," Lashay patted Jessica on the back as she released her from the hug.

"No, I look at all of you and just can't help but wonder. I mean, you all are so beautiful and strong. I want to know how you got to this place," Jessica firmly hugged Lisa.

"Jessica, that will take several more hours to tell, but let me leave you with this. God is a keeper!" Kory was the last to give Jessica a heartfelt hug.

"I'm going to go start some coffee and make some sandwiches. Jessica, feel free to let your family in. I know you are excited to see them," Kory disappeared back into the kitchen. Lashay joined Kory in the kitchen to give her a hand. As the doorbell rang, Jessica jumped up to open the door. She took a final breath and turned the knob to pull the door open. Jessica's father introduced himself before rushing to grab his baby girl in his arms. Lisa quickly made her way into the kitchen to allow the love to overflow between Jessica and her family. After all of the formalities and formal greetings, it was time for our new baby sister to leave. The tears we saw in Jessica's emerald eyes earlier in the evening we're not the same ones she was now shedding. The three remaining grandmothers stood together in the window and waved goodbye.

Deep down we knew this would not be the last time we would see Jessica. Our emotions were happy but sad Jessica was gone. She was out of sight but not removed from our hearts. God gave us the opportunity to share our life lessons with someone who was going through their own. It doesn't matter age or ethnicity. Life is good. Life can be difficult. Life be lifing. There is nothing new under the sun. When you feel you are the only one, as you meet people, you will always find others, that have been through it as well. We know not the road we travel or who we'll meet along the way. Just know, along the road, will be lessons each and every day.

Eight months later at the grandmother's monthly girl's night out, there was several hard knocks at the door.

"Dang who is beating on my door," Kory frowned, wiping her hands on the front of her apron. She and Lashay walked into the living room to see what the ruckus was about.

"I'll get it," Lisa yelled out. Lisa pulled the door open and her eyes traveled down to the diaper bag sitting on the ground to the person standing in front of her holding something in her arms.

"Surprise! Am I late? Did I make it in time for dinner?"

The three grandmothers stood with their mouths wide open in shock and excitement.

NOTES:

DISCUSSION QUESTIONS

1. What is your definition of a friend? Has your definition of a friend changed over the years?

2. Are you giving and putting into your friendships the same that you expect to receive back?

3. What are things that we share in common as women of all races?

4. Would you help if you saw someone in need like Jessica? Why or why not?

5. Each character had a means to escape challenging seasons in their lives to free themselves from hurt and pain. How do you escape? What are you trying to escape or free yourself from?

6. Camille often self-medicated with herb and her best friend's man. What or who do you turn to as a coping mechanism?

7. An old saying like Kory's grandmother used to say is "Thank God I don't look like what I've been through." If I were to look at you today, what would I be surprised to know you've been through in the past or are currently going through today?

8. Have you had a bad experience with an organization or a group that was considered a safe space but left you vulnerable and hurt? For example, Kory experienced hurt in the church setting.

9. How did you heal from the hurt or are you still in the process of healing?

10. Have you had a slow dance experience like Lashay? Does slow dancing and the art of intimacy without sex still exist today?

11. Have you ever been disappointed to find out the perfect couple in your eyes really had a lot of issues? Did it discourage you about relationships? For example, how Lashay viewed her parents and her aunt and uncle.

12. Do you know of married couples who sleep in separate beds? Is it a good idea to bring this practice back?

13. Lisa experienced heartfelt trauma by the absence of her father in her life. Can you relate to her or do you have daddy issues?

14. Does the role a father plays in one's life have an effect on our relationships and friendships?

15. Have you ever made an agreement or arrangement with someone to benefit yourself and help you move forward? After things progressed, were you ashamed or even sorry for your actions?

16. How was your sex talk? Was it with your parents, friends, or did you have to figure it out on your own?

17. Were you misinformed about sex?

18. When was the last time you took a step back to enjoy and embrace the simple things in life, like from your childhood?

19. Can you handle the truth once it's been revealed? What did you do? Did you pray, call someone, hire a lawyer, or handle things your way?

20. Sexual abuse is never the fault of the person who was taken advantage of and abused. What can we do to help others heal who have had traumatic experiences in their lives?

21. Have you ever experienced colorism or has the complexion of one's skin made a difference in how a person was perceived or received?

NOTES:

About the Authors

Kimberly Perry Allen is a playwright, writer and co-author to the new novel, "Life Lessons." She was born and raised in Louisville, Kentucky. A mother and grandmother, she enjoys spending time with family and friends. Drawing strength from her own experiences, Kim finds significance in writing about social issues faced by women of color. Over the years, she has become an advocate for individuals with special needs and mental illness and those that care for them.

Kimberly is currently working on a historical novel, closely based on her family history that chronicles the love story and journey between a Native American Cherokee and her African enslaved husband.

Jacqueline Goodwin, a Child of God. Among her many important titles are Wife, Mother, Grandmother and now Author. She considers it a blessing to be on this new journey with her co-authors. Always trusting and believing in God's holy word.

"When you pass through the waters, I will be with you; and when you pass through the rivers, they will not sweep over you. When you walk through the fire, you will not be burned; the flames will not set you ablaze." Isaiah 43:2

Teena Saunders currently resides in Louisville, Kentucky. She is a mother of two and a grandmother of three.

"But I do not account my life of any value nor as precious to myself, if only I may finish my course and the ministry that I received from the Lord Jesus, to testify to the gospel of the grace of God." Acts 20:24 (ESV)

Resource List

Suicide and Crisis Line 988

National Domestic Violence Line 800.799.7233

Sexual Assault Hotline 800.656.4673

Treatment for Mental Health Hotline 888.545.9116

Drug Abuse Hotline 406.602.0539

Autism Speaks www.autismspeaks.org

National Cancer Support (888) 793-9355

Life's Lessons
Living and Loving Leaving No Stone Unturned
Playlist

If our Story had a soundtrack this would be the playlist
Listen, dance, and reflect on our story through music
(We do not own the rights to these songs)

Introduction
"Life and Favor" by John P Kee

Girls Night Out
"Not Tonight (Ladies Night remix)"
by Lil Kim feat. Missy Elliot, Left Eye, Da Brat, Angie Martinez, Queen Latifah

White Picket Fence
"Meeting in the Ladies Room" by Klymaxx
"Mary Jane" by Rick James

Granny Used to Say
"Mama Used to Say" by Junior

Marriage to Me
"When We Get Married" by Larry Graham
"At Last" by Etta James

So…God Made Sex Beautiful
"You're the Best Thing that Ever Happened" by Gladys Knight

You Doing Too Much
"Secret Lovers" by Atlanta Starr
"Circles" by Atlanta Starr
"When Love Calls" by Atlanta Starr

Two Wrongs Don't Make a Right
"Woman to Woman" by Shirley Brown
"In My Bed" by Dru Hill
"Enough Crying" by Mary J. Blige

Slow Dancing
"Reasons" by Earth Wind & Fire
"Slow Jam" by Midnight Star
"Nobody's Supposed to Be Here" by Deborah Cox

Memories of the Way We Were
"Memories of the Way We Were" by Barbara Streisand
"Daddy's Song" by Carl Thomas

What You Do It For?
"Let's Talk about Sex"- Salt and Pepper
"P.Y.T. (Pretty Young Thing) by Michael Jackson

Country Memories
"Tennessee" by Arrested Development
"Po Folks" by Nappy Roots and Anthony Hamilton

Looking Back
"Break Every Chain" by Tasha Cobb
"Way Maker" by Sinach

Missing My Mother
"You Don't Own Me" By Grace featuring G-Eazy
"Hurt" by Christina Aguilera

Full Circle
"The Circle of Life" by Carmen Twillie and Lebo
"Get Here" by Oleta Adams

www.ingramcontent.com/pod-product-compliance
Lightning Source LLC
Chambersburg PA
CBHW050354030726
47503CB00006B/1848

* 9 7 8 1 9 5 9 5 4 3 9 3 0 *